THE MOUNTAINS OF ARARAT

A Novel

Aaron Simms

ISBN: 0692769021
ISBN-13: 978-0692769027

Published by St. Polycarp Publishing House
stpolycarppublishinghouse.com
info@stpolycarppublishinghouse.com

Printed in the United States of America
* * *

ABOUT THE AUTHOR

Aaron Simms is an author and writer specializing in Christian theology, history, and classical studies. He is also a pastor in The Lutheran Church – Missouri Synod.

His website is at:

www.aaronsimms.com

Dedicated to my wife and children, thank you for your love and support.

CHAPTER ONE

Prologue

Upon my return from my adventure, I was urged by my friends and family to write down a detailed account of all that had transpired. I resisted at first, thinking myself not up to the task. However, after much exhortation, they eventually prevailed upon me. Therefore, what follows is a true narration of my expedition to search for Noah's Ark in the Mountains of Ararat. I will not reveal the outcome here, but instead simply state that it was the journey of a lifetime which I hope the reader will enjoy through the conduit of my written words.

- John Welz

CHAPTER TWO

The Waters

Noah's Ark. What a perplexing subject. In the Biblical book of Genesis, the Ark was the ship on which Noah and his family survived the flood which God sent upon the earth. The flood itself was one of the major events recorded in the book of Genesis, after the original creation and before the Exodus of the Israelites from Egypt. The flood impacted the entire world and was, in essence, a recreation of sorts. The world had grown so sinful and had so rejected God that He decided to destroy it with water. However, He graciously saved a remnant whom He accounted as righteous.

The Bible records:

The LORD saw that the wickedness of man was great in the earth, and that every intention of the thoughts of his heart was only evil continually. And the LORD was sorry that he had made man on the earth, and it grieved him to his heart. So the LORD said, "I will blot out man whom I have created from the face of the land, man and animals and creeping things and birds of the heavens, for I am sorry that I have made them." But Noah found favor in the eyes of the LORD (Genesis 6:5-8).

Thus, the existing world was wiped away in the waters of the flood, and only Noah and his family - eight people - were saved, along with the animals which God had them bring onboard their ship. The Bible records that Noah and his wife had three sons - Shem, Ham, and Japheth - and these sons each had a wife. It was only this one family of eight people which were saved from the flood. After the flood waters subsided they, and the animals with them, departed the Ark and started a new life in a world which had been cleansed with the waters, beginning the process of repopulating the world and filling it with life.

All major ancient world cultures have similar stories as that recorded in the Bible. They had memories of a flood or of the world emerging out from the waters. Were these echoes of the Biblical truth? The Egyptians speak of the world being created after a flood. The Aborigines in Australia and the Native Americans have flood stories, as do the ancient Greeks, Hindus, Mayas, and many others. The most famous and well known - outside of the Bible - is the Gilgamesh epic of Mesopotamia. Many believe that it is the most closely parallel account of a global flood as that recorded in the book of Genesis. The story of the flood which is detailed by the Bible is echoed in the ancient texts of these other cultures as well. It is as if the descendants of Noah, as they repopulated the earth, carried the memory of the flood with them, distorting it with time until God gave Moses and the Israelites the correct account, which Moses recorded in Genesis.

Despite the importance of the Ark to this shared history of the world's cultures, though, no one has ever found it. This even though it is arguably the main character in the flood story apart from Noah. Without the Ark there would be no salvation and Noah would have perished in the flood. For such a prominent, grand artifact to have been lost for so long is hard to believe. Yet, it has never been found. Certainly, there have been people over the years who had claimed to have found it, even astronauts and famous explorers, but no definitive proof has ever been presented. It is fascinating that such a reportedly large ship, given the dimensions in Genesis, has remained elusive for millennia. How has it remained hidden? Where is it?

The answer to these questions intrigued me throughout my life. My main hobby, since I remember even having a hobby, was researching Noah's Ark and speculating on its final resting place. As a kid, I had poured over printed maps of the area around Armenia, Azerbaijan, Turkey, Iran, and Iraq - looking for likely mountains where the Ark may have landed. Later, I switched to computerized maps and software to continue the search. Whatever books I could find on the topic, whatever reports from the region, I read.

* * *

I have other interests as well, certainly. I enjoy ancient, or classical, history. As a child, I had read Julius Caesar's *Gallic Wars* and *Civil War*. Later, I read Thucydides *Peloponnesian War* and Livy's *War with Hannibal*. Also, Herodotus' *Histories*, Pliny the Elder's *Natural History*, and others of the theme. I was well versed in classical history and probably a bit precocious and odd as a child as a result. There was just something about reading these histories which was exciting. It was like being transported back in time and living in them for a while.

These histories told not only of great deeds and perilous times, but also of the human condition which has been remarkably consistent throughout history. In Thucydides, for instance, there is the classic line of the Melian Dialogue: "The strong do what they will, while the weak do what they must." In Livy, there's the epic contest between the Roman Republic and the Carthagnian Empire which culminates in the final clash on the plains of Zama between the Roman armies of Publius Cornelius Scipio "Africanus" and the Carthaginian armies of Hannibal Barca. In Caesar's writings, he tells of his conquests against his enemies as well his strategy for winning. The books of Herodotus and Pliny speak of fascinating and exotic peoples and animals. The lesson of these books, and those like them, is that if a person wants to know more about himself and his society, a good place to start is by reading about those who have come before him.

* * *

In addition, and in a similar vein, I enjoyed studying the history of the Christian Church. In particular, I had always been interested in the first few centuries of the New Testament Church, reading writings from men such as Clement of Rome, Clement of Alexandria, Polycarp, Justin Martyr, Irenaeus, Ignatius, Tertullian, Origen, and Augustine, among others of their times. Similar to how a person can gain a better appreciation for the human condition through reading history, which I've mentioned above, I've also found that one can acquire a deeper appreciation of the Christian faith by reading the writings of those who were instrumental in its earliest years. For Christian apologetics I went to writers such as Justin Martyr and Tertullian. For an exposition of the faith: Ignatius, Irenaeus, the two Clements, Polycarp. For just about anything, including a personal confession of his own journey to faith (which I found refreshing and comforting): Augustine. The Christian faith of our own time rests upon the shoulders of those who have argued about it and expounded upon it prior to us.

All this is a long way of saying that Noah's Ark fit nicely into that intersection of history and the Christian faith which most interested me. It was as if my two main threads of passion met each other in the Ark. It was an emblem of God's actions within history, a point where He intervened both to judge sin as well as save His people.

Where is the Ark now, though? It is certainly hard

to determine where it even might be. The first major problem with locating it is that the Bible doesn't give the exact location where Noah and his family disembarked. It simply says:

At the end of 150 days the waters had abated, and in the seventh month, on the seventeenth day of the month, the ark came to rest on the mountains of Ararat. And the waters continued to abate until the tenth month; in the tenth month, on the first day of the month, the tops of the mountains were seen (Genesis 8:3-5).

The "mountains of Ararat." This is perhaps the key phrase in locating the Ark. Maybe the phrase "the tops of the mountains were seen" is important also? There is actually a modern "Mount Ararat" near the conjunction of Turkey, Armenia, Azerbaijan and Iran. It is within Turkish territory and consists of two main peaks: "Greater Ararat" and "Lesser Ararat." Both are extinct volcanoes; the Greater one rises to 16,854 feet and the Lesser to 12,782 feet - very high above the earth.

As a kid I had hiked to Grays Peak in Colorado, which has an elevation of 14,278 feet. We had to leave very early in the morning to reach the Peak before bad weather rolled in, and the sheer elevation and resultant thin air winded me many times as I trekked the ten mile route up to and back down from the peak. On a related note, because of that adventure I learned to understand why the Bible speaks of people "going up to Jerusalem." Jerusalem is on a plateau over 2,400 feet above sea level. That is not very high, but compared to the basically sea level elevation of much of the surrounding country, it is quite an elevation change. One goes "up to" the city.

At any rate, I had gone "up to" Grays on that day in my youth and never forgot it. How much more difficult would it be to go up to the "mountains of Ararat" to look for the Ark among the Greater and Lesser Peaks, even if these were actually the right mountains? Other cultures and countries have claimed that the Ark lies within their territory as well. Thus, the Ark could easily be on any number of other mountains in the region, or none at all - either because it has been lost to time or because it never existed, as the skeptics maintain. Nevertheless, the thought of finding it had always intrigued me.

Life, however, had gotten in the way of any thought of trying to go to Turkey or anyplace else to look for it. I really never seriously considered going. After all, I was married, had a family, a good job. Not to mention the fact that the entire area is not conducive for traveling: it is not exactly welcoming to Americans, it has been plagued by war for centuries, and the mountains are high and covered by snow. It was too high of a dream and too difficult a journey to seek out the Ark.

Therefore, I never thought I'd have the chance to go look for the Ark, but I suppose that life takes you places where you never thought you would be. I had planned to live a quiet, relatively relaxed life. Go to college, get a good job, get married, save some money, retire, grow old, die. That was my plan, especially the retirement part. Oh, how I had spent many hours calculating my savings and juggling my investments, all in the hopes of getting to an old age which was comfortable and leisurely. I just wanted to ride out life in tranquility and ease.

But, it was not to be. Thankfully.

Certainly, I did accomplish some of my plan. I did go to college, I did get a good job, I did get married to a lovely wife and have children. But, I haven't yet grown old (I don't think), nor have I died (thank God). But, my straight path to retirement and old age was interrupted by circumstances. I would indeed have the adventure of my lifetime first, before continuing with my other plans.

It was a Tuesday; I distinctly remember the exact day. I had returned home from work with the expectation of spending time with my family and enjoying a relaxing evening with them. Little did I know that events had already happened far away that would set me on a course which would forever change my life. This was the day everything changed. All due to an earthquake many thousands of miles away.

CHAPTER THREE

The Earthquake

I had just arrived home and was standing at the kitchen counter, leafing through the day's mail. Bills, junk mail, mail for the family who used to live here prior to us. Nothing too exciting, but for some reason I always looked forward to the mail arriving. I suppose it was the excitement of the unknown. Anything could come in that little mail truck to my house. Most often, though, it was simply the usual array of unremarkable parcels.

As I finished flipping through the mail we had received, my wife called out to me from the family room, "John, have you seen the news?" I hadn't. I wondered what had happened. Had there been another terrorist attack somewhere? Those seemed to occur much too frequently lately. Indeed, the news was normally depressing, so I did not often watch it.

"No," I answered as I went over to where Elizabeth was standing in the other room, watching the evening news on the television. There was a reporter in Turkey discussing a major earthquake, 7.2, which had hit the area. Thousands of people were dead, more missing, and many towns suffered extensive damage. This was all awful, but I still didn't know the real reason for why she had called me over to see this. I felt empathetic towards the people in Turkey, but wasn't sure that this was the purpose for which Elizabeth had summoned me.

"Wait for it," she said, "maybe they'll repeat it again."

"What?"

"Just wait. Here… listen."

The reporter was now interviewing a member of the Turkish military who explained that the earthquake had caused rockslides in the mountains and warning people to stay away from the area, due to the unstable ground. The epicenter of the quake, and thus the major damage, was near the Turkish border with Iran on the extreme eastern extent of Turkish territory. The nearby mountains of Ararat were affected, with new fractures and fissures opened in the rocky slopes.

"That's interesting," I said.

"Yes, but there's more."

The reporter then explained that the local people

in the area were reporting that - from the plains below the mountains - they had seen a large object situated high up in the mountains of Ararat; it had apparently been uncovered by the earthquake. Due to the movement of the rock and the resultant landslides, the snow which normally covered the area was disturbed, and the locals believed that, from a distance, they could see an object embedded in a rocky chasm which had been revealed by the earthquake. What it was exactly, though, no one could tell for sure. Due to the danger and general inaccessibility of the area no one had gotten close enough to see.

"They're speculating that it could be Noah's Ark," Elizabeth finally explained.

"Hmm, I wonder if someone will mount an expedition up there to take a look," I pondered aloud. "It's a fairly high elevation and it's already September, so the weather will be turning bad soon in the area. There's a good chance that whatever the locals think they see will be covered again soon by snow."

Elizabeth turned to me smiling, "You have to go for it."

"What?" I didn't follow. I was still thinking about the locals' reports and wondering what it was they saw. It could have been anything, even a shadow created by the rocky slopes of the mountains. I wasn't making sense of what Elizabeth meant.

* * *

"You have to go to Turkey to see if you can find it. You've been obsessed about this thing your whole life. You have to go. It may be your only opportunity. In fact, it may be the only chance for anyone, and you're the best one to go look for it. You've studied this thing for a long time and must know more about it than anyone else."

Go look for the Ark? The thought of it was crazy, and I told Elizabeth as much. As she stood there smiling at me, I started to think about it more fully. It truly was a once-in-a-lifetime opportunity and would be an incredible adventure and an amazing experience. My thoughts wandered over the sea to the mountains where I imagined myself walking up the slopes and encountering the Ark. It would be the find of the century, of the millennium even.

My thoughts then returned to home and my present situation where reality kicked in again. There's just too much going on here for me to head to a foreign land to look for something which may not even be there. My responsibilities with my work and family keep me here. How can I take off enough time from work to mount an expedition to the mountains in Turkey? How could I leave my family for a few weeks to go do this? Especially for what is more than likely a fool's errand.

I explained all of this to my wife. She listened patiently, but then reminded me of all the research I had done, all the maps I had studied, all the satellite footage I had poured over. Most importantly, she reminded me of the importance of taking the chance when presented with an opportunity which will not repeat itself, even when the outcome is unknown.

"And you can take Martin with you," she said.

Martin is our college-age son. She wanted both of us to go? I started to wonder if my wife just wanted us out of the house so that she and our high school daughter, Anna, could have time alone without "the guys." Or, she had completely lost her mind. To go to the border of Turkey, Iran, and Armenia by myself seemed crazy. To take our 20 year old son with us seemed crazier still.

We talked it over some more, and she impressed upon me the importance of a son and his father having a life-changing experience together, especially one such as this. The bond we would form would be unique and hard-won. Martin could take a semester off of college, and I could take a leave of absence from work; together we can go into the great unknown to look for something that has been lost for 4,000 years.

And so that's what we did.

CHAPTER FOUR

Preparation

If Martin and I were going to go on this adventure together, we first had to prepare. We began by heading to my study in the basement of our home in order to start working on the logistics of our journey. I had always adhered to the old adage attributed to General Omar Bradley, "Amateurs talk tactics, professionals study logistics."

There were two main areas which we needed to address in our logistical planning. First, we had to figure out what city and country to fly into in order to have the best chance of actually getting to the mountains of Ararat. The countries in the area were not known for welcoming Americans, so we hoped to avoid the more unfriendly locations while finding the shortest possible route to the mountains. Second, we had to plan out our gear and clothing we would bring with us for the expedition. We needed to pack for multiple climates and an unknown number of days, but minimize our luggage enough so that we could actually carry our packs while hiking up the mountains.

We really didn't have much time. With winter coming soon, we were racing against the clock - and the snow. We had to get to the mountains before we lost the window of opportunity afforded by the relatively milder weather of Fall, or someone else found what the locals believe they saw. If we were going to proceed on our expedition, we had to plan quickly and get over there as soon as possible.

Martin was excited to go. But, youth always is ready to charge in where experience is more reluctant to go. I, in my 40s and having seen how cruel and rough the world really is, was not quite ready for this trip, nor comfortable with thrusting my only son into the vagaries of the world. It would certainly be a different and more challenging experience than his present college life. We would be cold, hungry, tired. We would likely meet people who were not supportive of us being there or of us looking for the Ark.

"Martin, you know this is going to be difficult."

"Yes, Dad, I know. But, if we find it, we will be famous."

"Or infamous. If we find it. If we come back alive. Then, yes, maybe we'll be one of the two," I said. "That's all a big 'if.' We may not find anything at all. It could have been just rocks that the locals saw up on that mountain. In all the previous expeditions to find Noah's Ark, that's all that's been found. Just rocks; some which appeared superficially to be laid out like the hull of a ship, but rocks nonetheless. So, we may very well get all the way there and find…"

"Rock," laughed Martin as he completed my sentence. The thought of traveling all the way over to the mountains of Ararat and finding just rock was both humorous and disheartening at the same time.

"Yes, exactly. We may see some interesting rocks and nothing else. It could turn out to be just an expensive hiking trip. But, since we've already resolved to go, let's look at the maps. We won't know for sure what's there until we get there anyway, and we have to figure out how to get there first."

The earthquake's epicenter had been near the border of Turkey and Iran, close to the confluence of the borders of Iran, Turkey, Armenia, and Azerbaijan. It was slightly to the east of the mountains of Ararat which was our target. Obviously, we wanted to find a way to get to the mountains to explore the area in which the locals had reportedly seen the object. It was supposedly situated in the saddle between the two peaks of Greater and Lesser Ararat, on the north-eastern contour or leeward side of the slopes. The elevation was probably a good fourteen thousand feet in that area. We'd have a tough time at that altitude getting enough oxygen into our lungs, since we lived at a much lower elevation with much denser air. We needed to consider some acclimation time once we got there, before heading too high up.

The most direct route to the mountains would be to fly into Yerevan, the capital of Armenia, and then head south. The problem, though, was that there were no direct roads which could take us south; there were only two circuitous routes which would require around 12 hours to reach the mountains. Alternatively, we could fly to Ankara, Turkey and then travel overland by car for about 14 hours to the mountains. Both of these options therefore involved a long, arduous drive which would also increase the chances of us encountering problems. We could get picked up by the authorities or intercepted by terrorists. Iran and Iraq offered access into Turkey as well, but the prospect of flying into either of those countries was a non-starter; both were much too dangerous for Americans.

However, there was another more viable option: the city of Nakhchivan in Azerbaijan looked promising. It was an autonomous region of Azerbaijan having, as they say, "porous" border controls with the surrounding countries. It would be possible to get to the city of Nakhchivan by air and then drive overland about four hours into a sparsely populated thin sliver of Turkey which threaded the needle between the territories of Armenia and Iran. We'd need to get a car or maybe even a driver to help us cross the border into Turkey without attracting undue attention.

Once within Turkey, we could leave our car or driver and then approach the saddle of the peaks from the less populated north-eastern side of the mountain range. We'd hike south-west to the mountains and then up the slopes. This route seemed more manageable and offered a greater probability of actually getting to the mountain successfully. After weighing all the options, then, we chose this one; Nakhchivan would be our initial destination.

The first battle of our adventure, then, would be to get ourselves to Nakhchivan. Martin and I looked at flight options online and talked over our flight plan. There were a number of possibilities, with major European flight hubs in Amsterdam, Paris, and Frankfurt. After much discussion and searching, we decided to take a more indirect route to Nakhchivan to avoid undue attention from the authorities. We didn't just want to book a one-connection flight there. Therefore, we booked a series of one-way flights from Atlanta to New York, then on to Paris, one last connection in Istanbul, and finally to Nakhchivan. Our departure was in three days.

"We have to pack," I half-told, half-observed to Martin after we had settled on our flight plan.

"What do we need to bring?"

"Well," I said, " this will definitely not be like a normal weekend camping trip or a day hike. We'll need to bring a lot of gear to get us through our expedition, and I don't know for sure how long we'll be there."

I grabbed a pad of paper and started creating a list as Martin looked on:

- Hiking backpacks
- Tent
- Flashlights
- Batteries
- Clothing (multiple layers)
- Jackets and Coats
- Gloves
- Socks (multiple pairs)
- Water purifiers
- Iodine tablets
- Food rations
- Compass
- Binoculars
- Sunscreen
- Hats
- Fire starters
- Knives
- Canteens
- Shovels
- Pick axes
- Cooking pots and utensils
- Rope
- Cord
- Camera (with flash, SD card, and spare batteries)
- Maps

* * *

Thinking about the maps, I said, "I'll print up some topographic maps of the mountains which we can laminate and take with us. I have an old map pouch I can put them in, and I'll bring my grease pencils with us so we can mark them up as needed during our expedition. We can mark the places we've explored."

Martin nodded and then looked over the rest of list. "That's a lot of stuff."

"Yes." I considered the extent of the inventory for a moment. "We should probably pack most of it in a suitcase that we can check for the flights, and then carry on our backpacks with a few of the smaller items. Once we get to Nakhchivan we can reorganize everything for the expedition to the mountain. We should also bring something to read for the flights, and a notebook to record our expedition."

I think the gravity of the trip began to hit Martin. His face started to change from one of excitement to thoughtfulness. He asked quietly, "Dad, is it going to be dangerous?"

This is a hard question for a father to answer for his son. I respected him as a man and wanted to tell him the truth. Yet, he was still my son, and I felt the instinctual desire to try to protect him from the hard truth. The world was indeed a dangerous place, and if I had the power I would protect him from its dangers. Some day, though, he would be a man on his own, with his own family, and must be able to deal with the world as it is, not as we might wish it would be. In the end, then, I decided to be honest with him.

"Yes, son, it will probably be dangerous. First, there's the terrain. There's also the weather. Both of these will try to kill us on the mountain. And then there are people over there who don't much like foreigners, particularly us Americans." After a pause, I tried to reassure him, and myself, with the typical response of a father: "We'll be ok, though."

CHAPTER FIVE

On Our Way

The three days before our flights had passed very quickly. In the intervening time Martin and I had packed all our gear for the trip. We ended up having to go to the outdoor supply store to get a few items we were missing. I had an old tent already, but it was a six-person beast, so I bought a new, much smaller two-man pup tent. It would be lighter to carry and easier to pitch on the mountains. We also got the other items from our list which we needed. We also splurged a bit and bought new hiking backpacks. They were soft-framed packs with many MOLLE attachment points (like the military uses), so we could more easily mount equipment and supplies to the outside of the packs which we wanted to be able to access quickly and easily during our hikes. We would mount carriers for our canteens, snacks, flashlights, camera, binoculars, and maps there.

In these three days we also spent as much time with Elizabeth and Anna as we could, since we would be apart for quite some time. We had all gone out to dinner and to see a movie together as a family. Elizabeth and I also went on a "date night" without the kids. It saddened me to think about being away from them for so long, especially since I didn't know for sure when we would be returning. Martin would be ok; he was in college and of the age where he was spreading his wings and ready to be away from his family. I, on the other hand, had already lived through that stage of my life. At this point, I would really rather stay home with my wife and kids than go out on an adventure.

This would be no normal adventure, however. Only the Ark could propel me from my home to a foreign land to wander through cold mountains, looking for something which has not been seen for thousands of years. The odds of finding it, by my reckoning, were low. Nevertheless, it truly was a once-in-a-lifetime opportunity, as Elizabeth had pointed out to me.

"It's time to go, boys," called Elizabeth.

The time had come for Martin and I to leave our home and head out to begin our quest. Our flight to New York was scheduled for the early afternoon, and then our connection to Paris was later in the evening. Once we got to Paris we'd have one last connection in Istanbul before our final leg on to Nakhchivan.

Elizabeth and our daughter Anna would drop us off at the airport. They planned to spend the evening in the city, since it was a long drive to get there anyway. They had dinner arranged and would go see a movie together. It was good that they would get some "girl time," since Martin and I would have our own chance to bond during our trip. When we were all eventually reunited we would have to celebrate as a family again.

Martin and I lugged our suitcases and backpacks into the kitchen on the way to the garage. We were both wearing jeans and sweatshirts for the flight, planning to change into our hiking clothes only once we finally got to Nakhchivan. Our hiking clothes consisted of multiple layers of clothing made of rip-resistant materials, with a heavy coat for the outer layer. Our coats had multiple interior and exterior pockets to store important supplies which we needed to be able to access quickly, such as a compass, small flashlight, water purification tablets, and snacks.

I grabbed a glass of water to take in the car with me on the way to the airport, while Martin retrieved some snacks from the pantry. It would be the last full pantry we'd likely see for a while. I realized that I tended to take the ease of accessing food and clean water for granted. Only now that we were about to leave it behind did I start to appreciate just how relatively easy our lives really were. We had everything we could possibly need or want at our fingertips, or within a short drive to the store, or a short wait for the delivery truck. Once we got to the mountains, provisions would not be accessible with such ease.

We left the kitchen and went into the garage. Elizabeth opened the rear door of her SUV, and Martin and I stowed our luggage inside. Then, we all settled into the vehicle. Elizabeth drove, while I sat in the front passenger seat. Martin and Anna were in the back. It was good for us all to be together one last time, I thought. Who knew how long until we were together again?

This question was on Anna's mind as well. "When do you think you'll be back," she asked.

"We're not sure," I said. "It'll take us basically two days to even get there, another day will be spent getting to the mountains, and then we have to actually start our expedition. So, it's safe to say that it'll be at least a week, likely two. But, after two weeks we probably won't have enough food to stay out there any longer."

Elizabeth piped up, "You two be very careful and watch out for each other. Call me if and when you can and let me know how you're doing."

"I will. I'll call you from the airports as we make our way there. I'll also call once we get to our final destination. When we get to the mountains, though, I probably won't have a signal, so it may be a number of days until you hear from us after that."

"Ok, I love you," she said. "Be careful."

* * *

"I love you too, we will."

After about an hour, we arrived at the airport. Traffic was the usual Atlanta mess, but we made it. At least it would be nice to be away from traffic for a while, I thought. We won't likely hit any traffic jams where we're going. It'll also be nice to be away from a large city for a while and enjoy being outside. I hadn't gone hiiking or camping in quite a while, although this certainly would be unlike any other previous trip.

Elizabeth pulled up to the airport's departure terminal entrance to drop us off. She found a space in the line of vehicles and placed hers in park with the hazard lights on. Martin and I grabbed our gear from the back of the SUV and placed it on the ground so that we could hug the girls before we left. We were one of many families and friends saying goodbye today, as our story was being repeated by many others on the curb of the terminal. Nearby, a policewoman was urging cars along and blowing her whistle at those who lingered too long.

So it was that Martin and I said our final goodbyes to Anna and Elizabeth. It occurred to me then just how much I would miss them, especially my wife. She and I were not used to being apart for very long. I doubt that I would have gone on this trip had the potential prize not been so great. To find Noah's Ark was truly a once in a lifetime, or a once in many lifetimes, opportunity. Generations before me have wanted to find it and now it was my turn to go look for it. I would still miss my wife greatly, though.

After one last hug and kiss from our family, Martin and I grabbed our gear and headed into the terminal to check-into our flight and find our gate.

"Are you ready for this?" I asked him.

"Yes, how about you?"

"Ready as I'll ever be. Let's go."

We checked-in at the airline counter and handed over our checked luggage. We would both carry on our backpacks, but with minimal contents - just enough for the flight. Our plan was that once we got to our final destination, we'd repack our backpacks with only the gear we needed for the hike, placing everything else in our suitcases to leave behind. For the flight itself, we had simply brought some reading material and music to help us bide the time. I planned to sleep most of the trip, though.

Due to the way we had booked our flights, we'd have to retrieve our checked baggage in New York and again in Paris before checking-in for the next leg of our journey. This would be a bit of a hassle, but was the trade-off required for our decision to book single-leg flights, rather than an end-to-end flight to Nakhchivan. We did, though, book a connecting flight from Paris to Nakhchivan through Istanbul, so we would at least not have to pick up our luggage in

Istanbul.

Freed of our heavy luggage in Atlanta, it was much easier to make our way to the security area. We made it through security without incident, although I got selected for extra "random" screening. That is never fun; I always feel like the screener owes me dinner or something afterwards. Martin, half my age, wasn't selected. Figures.

Our flight was on time, so after milling around for another hour at the gate, we boarded the plane and lifted off for our adventure.

CHAPTER SIX

Arrival

Finally. It was a long series of flights, but we had made it to Nakhchivan International Airport. The initial flight from Atlanta to New York was easy enough. It was only a couple hours, and I was able to get some reading done. In the spirit of our adventure, I decided to re-read the book of Genesis, at least through to the flood account.

Genesis begins with the creation of the world when God speaks everything into existence. In fact, many people see the Holy Trinity in the opening chapter as the Father speaks His Word to create, and the Holy Spirit brings order to the creation. Thus, within the first few verses there are hints of the Father, Son, and Holy Spirit. As One God in Three Persons, they create and sanctify all that there is.

After creating the world, God forms Adam from the dust of the ground and Eve from the rib of Adam. He places them in a Garden and gives them everything freely, but forbids them to eat from one tree, the "tree of the knowledge of good and evil." There's nothing inherent in this tree which makes it this way; it's not a "magic tree" or anything like that. It is simply used by God as an instrument through which His people may worship Him. Adam and Eve, by obeying His command, demonstrate their trust in Him and thereby worship Him as their God.

Yet, Adam and Eve ultimately disobey God's command. They eat from the forbidden tree and as a consequence know evil. This rebellion against God brings sin, death, and evil into the world. It also causes them to be alienated from God, each other, and creation itself (since their bodies will one day die). Yet, God promises a Savior who will come to undue this Fall, removing its effects, and restoring creation to perfection. The rest of the Old Testament will continue to give hints of this Savior and provide more details concerning him.

Adam and Eve have a son, Cain, who they seem to think is this Savior. However, he is not; actually, far from it. Out of pride and anger, he later kills his younger brother Abel. Adam and Eve then have another son, Seth, and the promise of the coming Savior continues through Seth's line. In effect, God gathers together a people for Himself around this promise; this is the Old Testament Church. They are the people who trust in God and look forward to the arrival of the Savior.

Noah is descended from Seth. By his time, however, the world is thoroughly corrupt. The

Church has lost its faith, and there is much evil in the world. The Bible actually says:

The LORD saw that the wickedness of man was great in the earth, and that every intention of the thoughts of his heart was only evil continually. And the LORD was sorry that he had made man on the earth, and it grieved him to his heart (Genesis 6:5-6).

Therefore, God decides to destroy the world with a flood. The cleansing waters will remove the present corruption and evil from the surface of the earth. It is a Biblical truth that humanity's sin actually corrupts the land. This was seen in the original Fall of Adam and Eve into sin and is echoed much later during the time of the people of Israel when the Bible speaks of the ground itself being tainted by their sin. The coming waters of the flood will serve to wash the earth.

However, God has mercy on Noah and his family and therefore decides not to wipe them out with the flood. These eight souls - Noah, his wife, their three sons and their wives - are the entire Church on earth at the time. They will be preserved. Thus, God instructs Noah to build the Ark and carry onboard representatives of all the various kinds of animals. Noah does as God commands, the rains come, and the world is destroyed. Noah, his family, and the animals, however, are preserved. Eventually, the rains stop, the flood waters subside, and the Ark rests on the "mountains of Ararat." After Noah and his family disembark from the Ark, God gives them the sign of the rainbow as a promise to never again destroy the world through a flood. Noah and his family worship God and then begin to repopulate the earth, with the animals also dispersing out into the world.

The Savior - Jesus Christ - would ultimately come from Noah's son Shem (from which the word "semite" is derived), his descendant Eber (from which the word "Hebrew" comes), and their descendants Abraham, Isaac, Jacob, Judah (who gave his name to the Jews), Jesse, and David. The promise narrows over time until it is ultimately fulfilled in the person of Jesus Christ - the very Word of God come in the flesh - and then it widens through him to encompass salvation for all people. Without the Ark and God's preservation of Noah, though, none of this would have happened.

This Ark is what Martin and I were hoping to find. For now, though, we had ourselves occupied with getting to Nakhchivan so we could even begin our search. We arrived in New York with a three hour layover, so we found dinner in the airport, then boarded our next flight to Paris. The flight to Paris was a typical grueling overnight transatlantic flight. It wasn't long, only a little over seven hours. But, it was an awkward length; long enough to be uncomfortable, but too short to really get much sleep. I did my best to get as much rest as I could. But, by the time we got to Paris I was ready for the entire trip to be over; I really just wanted a good night's sleep in a comfortable bed. However, we still had a couple more flights before getting to Nakhchivan.

The layover in Paris was short, only an hour. Charles de Gaulle Airport has frustratingly small connection windows and an inefficient transport system. That, combined with the fact that we had to go through passport control and security screening meant that we barely made our flight to Istanbul. We managed to get to the gate with just minutes to spare before the boarding window closed. Once safely on the flight, we relaxed a bit. However, we still had one more city to travel to before finally boarding our final flight to Nakhchivan. I fell asleep again, which made the three hour flight seem to go by quicker.

I woke up as we were coming in for landing in Istanbul. After the plane arrived at the terminal Martin and I exited and made our way to the next gate for our final flight. After reaching our departure gate, I looked out the window to see if the plane had arrived and noticed that it was much smaller than the ones we had flown in on the previous legs of our journey; it was just a small regional jet. Since we had a few minutes to spare, we were able to eat a simple lunch near the gate prior to boarding the plane. I was very tired, but happy that in a few more hours we'd be at our destination and the flying portion of our journey would be over.

Finally, this last flight in our ordeal landed at

Nakhchivan International Airport. The airport was just to the east of the main city, across the Nakhchivanchay River. It was small, consisting of a single terminal and two runways. After we landed we had but a short taxi to the gate where we disembarked the plane onto a ladder leading to the tarmac. From there we entered into the terminal. The decor of the whole airport could best be described as "communist-chic." The airport was built in the 70's, and the general ambience of that era remained. It was like being transported back in time; I half expected Soviet soldiers to be patrolling the area.

After entering the terminal, Martin and I headed silently to the baggage claim. Our plan for the day was to stay at a local hotel for the night and then, on the following morning, enter into Turkey and head to the mountains. It was late afternoon now, so I was ready to get to our hotel and find something substantial to eat. We had eaten on the previous flights, but I had been on enough flights in my lifetime to get tired of airplane chicken. Our lunch in Istanbul was not very filling either.

Before getting some much needed rest and sustenance, we first needed to retrieve our bags and get through passport control.

As we walked through the arrivals terminal we heard very little English spoken, mostly Azeri and a smattering of Turkish and Russian.

"Try not to talk," I whispered to Martin.   "It would be better if we just try to blend in."

We attempted to remain as inconspicuous as possible and tried not to stand out.   We certainly didn't want to broadcast "Americans" to everyone. So, we walked silently to baggage claim and waited as bag after bag dropped onto the conveyor belt and passed by us. I was so tired that the act of watching the bags drop was strangely mesmerizing. It was like playing the lottery; when would my bag be the one? Finally, my and Martin's bags appeared on the conveyor. I was elated.

We retrieved our bags and headed to passport control.   It was in a small corridor of the terminal. Our adventure lay just beyond. All we needed was a stamp from the passport official and we would be on our way.   The alternative would be to be denied entry into the country and sent back home: no adventure, no chance of finding the Ark. I hoped for the best as Martin and I got in line. The line was short, apparently not many people were wanting to go to Nakhchivan today.

When it was our turn, we proceeded together to the passport control desk and handed our passports to the official. He flipped through them, looked at us, looked at his computer screen, and then said something in, I assume, Azeri. I, politely as I could, said, "I'm sorry, I don't speak Azeri." He frowned, and didn't reply. I paused and then said, "Govorite po-Russki?" I had switched to Russian, which I had learned in college. I hoped that we could communicate in this way.

My question to the official had been, "Do you speak Russian?" "Da," - yes - he replied. Then, he asked me the purpose of our visit. Family hiking vacation, I explained in Russian. He paused, then shrugged and finally stamped our passports and waved us through. Apparently, he wasn't too curious about why we had traveled so far for a hike. I also was not curious about his lack of curiosity. I was just happy to be officially in the country so that our expedition could finally begin.

CHAPTER SEVEN

The Car

I had previously arranged for a car service to pick us up at the airport and take us to the hotel. As Martin and I walked to the ground transportation exit of the terminal I hoped that our driver would actually be there to meet us. Who knew if my internet reservation from America for a car and driver in Azerbaijan would really be successful? I wasn't sure what we'd do if it wasn't. I was so tired and hungry that I just hoped for a quick and easy trip to our hotel.

We exited the terminal and looked through the few drivers who stood there with handwritten signs containing last names. Most of these guys I would not want to get into a car with; they all seemed fairly unsavory. After scanning a few of them, I found a man holding a handwritten sign which said, "Welz" - our last name. He was of average height - must have been about 5 foot 10 or so - and looked to be in his mid-40's. His face was weathered and tanned. Thankfully, he - as promised by the booking agency I had used - spoke English.

Walking up to him I said, "Hello, I am John Welz and this is my son Martin."

He nodded and smiled. "I am called Arman. My car is parked just outside."

We shook hands and then followed Arman out of the terminal into the parking lot. He led us to a small, gray, older sedan. As we approached, he unlocked the car and opened the trunk. He motioned for our bags which he placed into the trunk one-by-one as we handed them to him. Then, he closed the trunk, went around to the rear passenger-side door, opened it, and motioned for us to enter.

Martin and I slid into the rear seat of the car as Arman entered into the driver's seat. I could see that the otherwise empty front passenger seat was covered with papers, water bottles, and food wrappers.

"Would you like anything to drink?" he asked.

"No, thank you," I replied. "Here is the address to our hotel." I handed him a printed map with the hotel's address.

"Yes, I know it well. We shall be there in a few minutes."

He started the car and began driving. We exited

the parking lot and drove out onto the main access road which circled the airport. Arman's driving was typically erratic, like many cab drivers I had experienced previously in other parts of the world. He seemed to know exactly where he was going, though. He was likely a local who had lived here much of his life and who knew every nook and cranny of the town.

After getting onto the main road, Arman asked, "You here on business?"

"No," I answered. "Just a family vacation." I was trying to be circumspect.

"Oh? This is a strange place to go for a vacation, I should think, especially from America," he chuckled.

"Well, we've always wanted to see this part of Europe, and we thought we'd do a little hiking to see the countryside."

"I see. It is a beautiful place. I hope you enjoy your time here. I will have you at the hotel in a few minutes. You can rest and then begin your exploration of this amazing city."

As we drove along, he explained the history of Azerbaijan and pointed out the sights which passed us by as we proceeded along the road to the hotel. The civilization in the area goes back thousands of years, and the land has been occupied successively by the Medes, Persians, Armenians, various Muslim caliphates, the Turks, and finally the Soviet Union from which it achieved its independence in December 1991. The current people inhabiting the land share a cultural and language affinity with the Turks. The Nakhchivan province where we were is unique, in that it is an autonomous republic of Azerbaijan with its own elected government. The country has a lot of corruption, but is relatively advanced and prosperous and a member of many international organizations. These and various other facts were imparted to us by Arman as we proceeded to the hotel. It certainly did seem like an interesting place, and he was obviously proud of it. It was the pride of a native son for his land.

All well and good, but we would only be here a day, I thought to myself. I would not get to see much of the city or country. Our main destination - the reason we had endured so many hours of air travel - was Turkey and the mountains of Ararat. In fact, I had already pre-booked the same car service to take us across the border tomorrow. It appeared that Arman would be our driver for that leg of our journey as well.

As we pulled up to the hotel, Arman asked, "I am to take you into Turkey in the morning?"

"Yes," I replied.

"To Aralik? You hike there?"

Arman was referring to a small town to the northeast of the mountains of Ararat, just a few miles west of the Armenian border. It was about a two hour drive from Nakhchivan. I had planned for Martin and I to be dropped off in the town since it was fairly near to Ararat. We could start our hike to the foothills of the mountains from there.

"Yes, we will hike in the mountains near there."

He thought for a moment. "I hear strange stories from those mountains. I have lived in this area most of my life, and I and my family have been up on those slopes many times."

"What do you hear?" I asked.

"The Turks in the area say that Nuh's ship landed there. The people here in Azerbaijan, though, say that Nuh landed at Gapyjiq, the 'ship-rock' as it is known in the Azeri language. There are rock drawings there. His tomb is here nearby as well."

"Oh, really?" Nuh was the local form of Noah's name. Arman was correct; the Azeris claim that his Ark landed in their country. The name "Nakhchivan" itself means the "place of descent" where they believe that Noah came down from the mountain upon which the Ark rested and then founded the city. The Turks, however, also have their own "place of descent" near Mount Judi near the border with Syria and Iraq. Of the two locations, the town of Nakhchivan was certainly closer to the two mountains of Ararat. However, it is easy to imagine that from the Turks' point of view, when Noah came down from the mountains onto the plain, it would be near Judi; from the Azeris' point of view it would be near Gapyjiq. Amazingly, what's in the middle of them if you look towards the mountains from each location? Mount Ararat! Surely, we must be headed to the right mountains, lying centrally as they were between the competing claims of the Turks and Azeris.

"I will take you there - to Nuh's tomb and the ship-rock," Arman said, seeming to insist. "We shall go to his tomb in the morning and then we can go see the drawings at Gapyjiq. Can you spare a day before beginning your hike in Turkey?"

Spare a day, I thought? To see Noah's purported tomb and ancient drawings on the rocks at Gapyjiq? That was an easy answer. "Yes, I think we can spend an extra day here in Nakhchivan, before our hike. Those sound like interesting sights to see. Thank you."

"It is settled. I shall pick you up in the morning at 8 as previously agreed, but take you to Nuh's tomb and then on to Gapyjiq where you can see the drawings which they say Nuh and his family carved there after the flood. Then the next day I will take you to into Turkey."

"Thank you, very much," I answered. Then we exited his car, retrieved our bags, and parted ways until the morning.

CHAPTER EIGHT

The Hotel

Martin and I entered the hotel through a set of glass revolving doors. It was a nice, modern, western-style hotel of what looked to be five stories. I was surprised, actually. In my mind, I had imagined some sort of run-down, cinderblock establishment. However, this hotel looked like it could have been in downtown Atlanta or any other American city. The floors were freshly washed tile, with a pleasing pattern of whites and tans. The walls were painted a soft yellow with wood, glass, and mirror accents; the ceilings were high with plenty of recessed lighting. The check-in counter appeared to be a natural-stained maple.

We went to the counter, and said "hello" to the desk clerk. She was dressed smartly in a skirt, white shirt, and dark blue jacket. She smiled at us and greeted us in English. She asked for our passports and for a credit card for the room charges, which I handed to her. As she was looking at our passports, I asked her if we could extend our stay an extra night.

This was no problem, she informed us. In fact, the hotel didn't seem to be very crowded and had plenty of vacancies. It definitely wasn't the high tourist season here.

She gave us two keys to our room: 307. She also wrote down the wifi password onto our room cards and instructed us that breakfast would be served starting at 6am in the dining room. She pointed out the dining room across the hall and the elevators which lay in the same direction. We thanked her and then lugged our bags to the elevator to head to our room. I had booked us a standard room with two single beds. It should be ok for a couple of nights - certainly much nicer than the following nights would be in the mountains.

We got off the elevator on the third floor and found our room. It was just a few doors down from the elevator. I unlocked the door with the electronic key card and entered. The room was laid out nicely; the bathroom was on the left as we entered, and the main room with the two beds was just beyond. I chose the bed closest to the bathroom, while Martin took the bed further away, nearest the window. There were nightstands next to each bed and a dresser on the opposite wall, upon which sat a fairly modern television. Inside the dresser was a mini-bar.

The view from the window of our room gave us a glimpse into the city. The city skyline was low, with few tall buildings. The immediate area of the city was flat, with mountains off in the distance. It reminded me of Anchorage, Alaska or cities like Denver or Salt Lake City, but on a smaller scale. The streets were wide, but with few cars. I could see a gas station and other hotels nearby, and houses in the distance. It was a typical small Eastern European town; about 75,000 people live here. There was also a mosque in view not far from the hotel. The sky was a cloudy gray today.

We set our luggage down on the floor by the wall across from the beds on either side of the dresser. We then both proceeded to get cleaned up for an early dinner. After such a long flight to get here, I was happy for the opportunity to rinse my face off. It cooled me down and helped me to feel so much better. I couldn't remember the last time I had brushed my teeth or shaved, either; it seemed like we had left so long ago. International travel has a strange effect on one's sense of time. I decided not to shave, though, figuring that a beard would help insulate my face from the cold weather on the mountains.

Before heading to dinner, we decided to re-shuffle our luggage and pack our hiking backpacks. We unpacked our suitcases and loaded our packs with the clothing and gear we would need for our trek to and up the mountains. We'd re-wear our jeans tomorrow and then pack everything in the suitcases which we didn't need for the hike. Our backpacks were meant for the essentials to help us survive on our expedition, along with our flashlights, cameras, and notebooks. I also had a small pocket-sized Bible which I had always liked to carry in my jacket or coat pocket while hiking.

After finishing packing, we headed down to the restaurant to eat. By now I was starving and curious to see what they offer for dinner in Azerbaijan. The hotel restaurant had both an inner and outer entrance, so that both hotel guests and the general public could easily enter to eat there. We entered, of course, through the hotel-facing door of the restaurant. The decor was very modern. The floor consisted of light hardwoods, while the white walls were embellished with portraits of what must have been local famous people. I assumed that they were known to the Azeris, since I didn't recognize any of the portraits.

We were were greeted and then seated at a small table and handed menus by a pleasant hostess who spoke English. After seating us, she excused herself to go get us glasses of water and some fresh bread. Looking at the menu I saw a selection of typically Eastern European dishes: borsch, dumplings, potatoes, fish, rabbit, beef, even bear. The menu was printed in English, Azeri, and Russian. After a few minutes, our hostess returned, and I ordered a steak with potatoes (how much more American could I be?); Martin ordered a fish platter with dumplings. I hadn't had borsch since I was a kid, and wasn't in the mood for it again in my lifetime. Martin and I also ordered beers for ourselves - a reward and comfort for our long travels. It would be the first of a few that evening.

* * *

"How's Mom?" Martin asked. I had called my wife earlier from our room while Martin got cleaned up. I wanted to let her know that we had finally arrived safely.

"She and your sister are fine. They're going to do some redecorating around the house while we're gone. I suggested they try to go see a couple movies and go out to dinner some also. We shouldn't have all the fun."

Martin chuckled. I'm sure he was wondering the same thing I was: what would our house look like when we got back?

We chatted some more, then our food arrived. Tonight and the next night would be the last good meals we'd have for a while, since we would soon be embarking on the main part of our quest. My dinner was very good, but I was sure that after being out in the mountains for a while my return dinner would taste even better. There's nothing like eating a good hot meal after camping or hiking for a few days. We get so used to being able to have what we want, when we want it, that doing without for a while helps us to better appreciate what we have. I reflected upon the fact that being away from my wife, even for this short amount of time so far, has made me better appreciate how much I love her and our daughter and enjoy spending time with them.

I looked at Martin. It was great for us to be able

to do this together as father and son. I had been able to go on camping trips with my father when I was young, but once I went to college those sorts of father-son adventures stopped. I felt fortunate to be able to share this adventure with my own son. What an adventure it would be!

After we finished our meals, Martin asked, "What do you think of our driver?"

"He seems like an interesting fellow," I answered. Then, I pondered the things which our driver had said. "Kinda funny that he mentioned Noah."

"Yes, it was. He says that Noah landed near here, though, and not in Turkey."

"And the Turks," I observed, "claim Noah landed in their territory, as do the Arabs, actually. Everyone wants to have him as their own. I think it is only natural that each local people group in this general part of the world would think that Noah landed on their highest mountain before coming down onto the plains where their towns are located. It's also interesting that Mount Ararat is at the point of triangulation between these various claims of the Arabs, Turks, and Azeris. But, we'll see what our driver has to show us in the morning. I'm looking forward to seeing the purported tomb and the rock drawings."

After enjoying the last drops of our beers we headed back to our room for bed, awaiting our tour in the morning, courtesy of our driver Arman.

CHAPTER NINE

The Tour

Martin and I both woke early the next morning to prepare for Arman's promised tour of the city's landmarks related to Noah. I nearly fell out of the bed when I woke up; I wasn't used to sleeping in a single bed, not since college. My alarm had gone off, and I rolled over to turn it off and just about ended up on the floor. I had slept well enough during the night, but still felt groggy due to the time change. Martin got up as well, and we both dressed in the same clothes we had worn the day before. We hadn't planned on staying here an extra day, so our only other clothes were meant for hiking. I figured no one would notice or care.

We went downstairs to eat breakfast in the hotel's dining room. They offered a nice buffet with sliced deli meats, breads, various jams, boiled eggs, and fruit. In addition to the food, I guzzled a few cups of coffee to help wake myself up. Martin and I finished our breakfast and then returned to our room to grab my camera so that I could take pictures during our tour. When we were ready, we headed outside to be picked up by Arman.

As we waited for him outside the hotel, I enjoyed the fresh air. After being cooped up on airplanes for most of the last couple of days, it was refreshing to be outside. I could see the mountains in the distance with the sun just beginning to shine above the horizon, with a few wispy clouds in the sky. The breeze at this hour of morning was cool and comfortable, but the high temperatures in this area approached the mid-80s this time of year, which seemed surprisingly warm to me. However, I knew that once we finally got to the mountains of Ararat, particularly as we made our way up the slopes, the temperature would drop to below freezing. These extreme temperature changes had made packing somewhat more difficult. We would have to carry clothing with us for both warm and cold - extremely cold - weather.

Today would be an easy day, though. We were remaining in the area around Nakhchivan, being shuttled around by Arman to see the landmarks he wished to show us. There would be no high mountains, hiking, or cold today. We'd go with Arman to see the sights, then head back to the hotel to get some rest before our big adventure, slightly delayed, begins the next morning. In a way Arman's offer was well-timed; it would be nice to have an additional day of relative rest after our travels before having to hike up the mountains to look for the Ark.

* * *

As I admired the scenery, I caught a glimpse of a car I recognized. It was Arman. He drove up to the hotel and leapt out of his car to greet us. He seemed very excited, eager for the opportunity to show off his native land to us Americans. Martin and I could not hope to meet his level of outward excitement; it was too early in the morning and we were still jet-lagged. Regardless, though, I did look forward to seeing what Arman had to show us.

"You are ready?" asked Arman, with a note of excitation in his voice.

"Yes," I said. Then, I chuckled a bit, "You seem to be looking forward to this."

He laughed. "Oh yes, I love to show my country to visitors. Especially the tomb of Nuh and the drawings of Gapyjiq."

"Thank you very much for taking us."

He then ushered us into his car, and we sped off.

After a brief drive we arrived at a monument which was situated just off the side of the road, with mountains in view as a backdrop. This monument was the supposed tomb of Noah. It was an eight-sided stone structure with a correspondingly-shaped pyramidal roof on top. The stones themselves were arranged in such a way as to create an abstract geometric pattern. On one of the eight facings of the monument there were steps which led up to a small doorway through which one could enter the tomb.

I thought that the fact that the monument had eight sides was interesting. Christ rose on the "eighth day" (that is, the first day of the new week); baptismal fonts have eight sides for this reason, since baptism is a "re-birth" into a new life with Christ. In addition, baptism itself - a passing through the waters - is associated with the flood of Noah in the Bible, particularly in St. Peter's First Epistle. The implication is that just as God saved Noah through the waters of the flood, so too does He save us through the waters of Baptism. Christians throughout the centuries have made this connection between baptism and the flood. It was amazing to see this connection in visible form here, so far away from home; within the architecture of this eight-sided monument at Noah's purported tomb lay significant Christian imagery.

Arman explained that the monument was built in the 8th century and has been maintained ever since that time. Underneath the eight-sided structure was a burial chamber in which Noah's body was thought to be buried. No one was allowed to explore within the chamber, however.

Martin and I looked around the monument and took some pictures. Whether or not it was truly Noah's final resting place, it was certainly an interesting site and ancient structure. We entered the monument through the stairs and saw a plaque, which Arman read for us. It simply marked the site as the tomb of the prophet Noah. Arman went back to his car, giving Martin and I a few minutes to look around in privacy; there was no one else at the tomb.

"Do you think he's actually in here?" asked Martin.

"I don't know," I said. "Not likely. Like I said last night, a lot of peoples - the Azeris, Turks, and Arabs in particular - claim that they have Noah's tomb and the location where his ship landed. Pious Christians and Muslims centuries ago sought to honor him and, in all honesty, probably truly believed that he was buried in their town. I doubt this is the actual place where his body is located. It is an impressive monument, however."

After we were finished looking around, we returned to Arman's car and got in.

"What do you think?" he asked.

"Very interesting. Thank you for taking us here," I answered.

"Yes, we are very proud of this tomb," he said.

"I can see why. You should be. It is very beautiful and historic."

* * *

Arman smiled. "There's more to see." He shifted the car into gear and headed off in order to take us to a mountain in the distance, Gapyjiq, to look at the rock carvings he had mentioned the day before.

After another short drive we arrived at our destination. We were able to get fairly close by following a well-worn dirt road. Arman parked the car and we got out to explore, walking the remaining distance by foot. Once we reached the boulders at the foot of the mountain we could clearly see that carved on them were many stylized pictures of animals and people. Some of the pictures were difficult to make out; obviously they had meant something to those who carved them, but the message was now unclear. We all marveled at the rock carvings and traded theories on what some of the particular images could be. It was great fun to speculate on the images.

According to Arman, the locals believed that Noah's ship landed on this mountain and that he and his family carved the images. They then went down to the plain to restart their lives as they began the task of repopulating the earth, founding the town of Nakhchivan in the process.

Then something extraordinary happened.

CHAPTER TEN

Unexpected

I had previously assumed that Arman was so excited because he believed these local legends and wanted to show them to us. Now, however, he shifted his tone. In a calm, quiet voice he turned to Martin and I and said, "Of course, this is not really where Nuh's ship landed."

"What do you mean?" I asked.

"Well," he said, "Nuh's ship landed in the midst of the mountains of Ararat to the west of here, in Turkey. The mountains here at Gapyjiq with their drawings may have been created by Nuh and his family after they founded Nakhchivan and began spreading out. However, their ship is not here - it is at Ararat. As I told you yesterday, I have been on the slopes of Ararat many times. I have heard the stories of the shepherds who live near there. They say that when the snow melts in hot years that they see things, things that look like part of a huge ship. I have never seen it myself, but I believe those who tell me this. The shepherds do not like to speak of it, because it attracts foreigners" - he paused - "such as yourself." He stopped again and seemed to be thinking. After a few uncomfortable seconds, he said, "You say you are to be hiking near there. Are you looking for Nuh's ship?"

I thought as fast as I could. Could I trust Arman? Was it any of his business? What would he do if I told him the truth?

"Why do you think we would be looking for it?" I asked the question as a delaying tactic to give me more time to think.

"You seem to have a lot of equipment to just go on a family hike. And, you doubtless have heard the recent news reports of something seen in the mountains after the earthquake. I myself believe that what was seen was Nuh's ship."

"Arman, I ask for your trust in what I am going to tell you. You must tell no one."

"Yes, of course," he said, seeming genuine in his response. I felt that I could trust him.

"My son and I are, in fact, here to look for the Ark of Noah as you have suspected. We heard of the earthquake and the reports of the object and decided to travel here to try to find the Ark. It would be the greatest archaeological find and serve to help demonstrate to the world that the flood of Noah really happened. It would also be a testament of God's power as well as a physical witness of his mercy to Noah. It has been a lifelong obsession of mine to find it, and I wanted to take the chance which presented itself of looking for it."

"It is an awfully big chance you are taking indeed, sir." He sounded somber.

"How do you mean?"

He continued, "The shepherds do not appreciate foreigners, and the Turks also do not like people poking about on the mountain. I myself am a Christian, but most around here are not. They consider the ground around the mountain holy to Islam and would not appreciate Americans there. There are also other threats: terrorists and rebels, not to mentions the mountain itself."

Martin and I were silent. None of this was really news to us. After all, we had considered all of this before we came here. But, hearing it from someone else, particularly a local, was sobering.

Finally, after an impenetrable silence in which the minds of all three of us were thinking through this unexpected turn of events, Arman piped up again. "You will not go alone, my friends," he said. "I will accompany you to protect you."

"Protect us? Please, Arman, you do not need to do that. You barely know us."

* * *

"That may be, my friend. But, if you and your son intend to go to the mountain, I will go with you. I can help you and I too would like to see Nuh's ship with my own eyes, if we are to find it. I shall take you into Turkey tomorrow as planned, but will go to the mountain with you as well. Tonight I will make preparation."

Martin and I looked at each other, both silently wondering if we should trust our new-found friend and what his ultimate purpose was. Did he intend to really help us, to protect and guide us? I did not know. I hoped so. Regardless, he now knew our secret, and we needed him to drive us into Turkey anyway. It would be helpful, I supposed, to have an extra person in our party.

Thus, supposing we had no choice, I resigned myself to this third member joining our expedition. "Alright," I said to him, stretching out my hand to shake his. "The three of us shall go together."

"Four," he said, "for I shall bring one of my sons as well."

His son too?! How on earth did we end up with two extra members of our expedition, I wondered? This was turning out to be quite the adventure indeed.

CHAPTER ELEVEN

Across the Border

After our little tour of the area ended, Arman dropped Martin and I off at our hotel. He bid us farewell and promised to pick us up the next morning at eight o'clock to begin our drive to Turkey, bringing his own son along with him. Martin and I headed straight to the hotel restaurant for dinner. We ate quickly, enjoying a hot meal and a couple last beers while we still had the opportunity before our expedition in the mountains commenced. We then returned to our room, wanting to get a good night's sleep since the next day would be a long one.

The morning arrived quickly. I had woken up a couple hours before Arman's expected arrival so that I would have time to eat breakfast, drink my usual load of coffee, and ensure that my pack was prepared for the trek into the mountains. I woke Martin at the same time so that he could get ready as well. He seemed to be more energetic than I was; of course, he was about half my age and still believed in his own invincibility. I, however, had lived enough of my life to have had that youthful sense of optimism nearly ground out of me.

Nevertheless, here I was in Azerbaijan - a place I never thought I'd be - about to embark on the greatest of adventures, and with my son at my side. The thought injected into me a sense of excitement and optimism. A day I never imagined would arrive had, in fact, arrived - seemingly with no forethought or planning of my own. It was as though I had stumbled onto this path, a path I did not choose and a path from which I could now not deviate. I imagined that I was on a train which had already left the station, carrying me with it. My inevitable intersection with destiny, or fate, or - more to my liking - the Divine awaited.

After eating breakfast and gathering our luggage and gear, Martin and I checked out of the hotel and walked outside. It was another cool, comfortable morning, but I knew that the day would grow hotter - into the 80s. We wore long pants and short sleeve shirts, leaving our coats tied around our packs. We would need them later; once we finally got up into the higher elevations of the mountains of Ararat the temperature would begin falling rapidly.

After a short wait outside, Arman pulled up to the hotel with his car, and he and a young man who I assumed to be his son got out to greet us.

"This is my oldest son Yezras," explained Arman,

motioning to him. He looked to be about the same age as Martin.

We all exchanged pleasantries and shook hands. Arman and Yezras helped us load our gear into the trunk of his car. We would leave our suitcases in the trunk during our hike, taking only our backpacks with the supplies we needed. I noticed that they had also brought their own backpacks, which I could tell were loaded with equipment. After storing our gear, we all piled into the car to begin our drive to the border with Turkey. The car had seemed larger yesterday, before we had overloaded it with four fairly large men and an accompanying assortment of hiking and camping gear. Yezras and Arman were in the front, Arman driving. Martin and I were in the back.

We were apparently all tired and full of silent thoughts, as no one said a word for the first few minutes of the drive. Finally, Arman broke the silence.

"We shall soon be at the border where we will cross. Once we are in Turkey we will head to the village of Aralik. We will leave the car there, then hike on foot to the south-west until we get to the foothills of the mountains. We should make camp there for the night, before heading up the slopes."

"Sounds good," I assented.

Arman continued, "One thing I must tell you, sir."

* * *

I have always hated it when someone says that they have to "tell me something." Whenever I hear that phrase I instinctively cringe and prepare myself for what is to come. Normally, it is not good news; no one prefaces good information.

Arman's news was indeed not good, confirming my presuppositions. "The mountains are dangerous, as I said. It is not just the weather and the rocks. It is the people. Most mistrust outsiders and there are also rebels and terrorists about. Yezras and I have come prepared."

As he said this, Yezras pulled out a canvas bag from under his seat. He then leaned back from the front passenger seat and opened the bag to show us what was inside. Martin and I leaned forward to take a look.

Inside were four handguns and loaded magazines.

"They are 9mm, CZ 75s," explained Yezras.

I was familiar with them. The CZ 75 is an iconic handgun, rivaling the Colt 1911 design in ubiquity and popularity. Whereas the 1911 is the quintessential American firearm, the CZ is a very popular firearm of the countries of the erstwhile Eastern bloc. Introduced in the former Czechoslovakia in 1975, it is still manufactured today in the Czech Republic and its design has been copied by countless manufacturers around the world.

Yezras and Arman's examples looked a little rough, but certainly serviceable. The blueing of the slides and frames was well-worn, and the grips had some dings in them; otherwise, they seemed to be in decent condition.

Arman continued his son's explanation. "We must carry them for protection in the mountains, but keep them hidden from the authorities. Yezras will conceal them under the seat until we cross the Turkish border and reach the town. Then, we'll pack them with us on our trek."

Martin and I exchanged knowing glances. We were foreigners essentially being illicitly conveyed into Turkey on false pretenses and now carrying firearms illegally. Yet, we both knew that these CZ 75s provided some insurance for this adventure. We had no idea who we might meet while on the plains around the mountain or up on the slopes. It was easy to forget, in our relatively comfortable lives back home, that there is much danger and evil in the world. It would be better to be prepared to meet it than to try to ignore its presence or put oneself at its "mercy."

I had always been interested in firearms, actually. Beyond the fact that they serve as an equalizer, allowing anyone to defend themselves against criminals and tyrants, their simplicity appealed to me. They were elegant instruments of chemistry and physics. By elegant I mean to say that they possess a rational, minimalist system of design in which every part serves a purpose and functions according to plan. The chamber holds a metallic cartridge consisting of brass casing, primer, powder, and bullet. A pull of the trigger causes either a hammer (in the case of the CZ 75) or a striker to push a firing pin against the cartridge's primer. The force of the firing pin ignites the primer. This in turn sets off the gun powder, creating gas which pushes the bullet out of the casing, down the barrel (receiving spin from the barrel's rifling in the process), and towards the target. Once the chamber pressure begins to drop, the slide is forced backward by the recoil, the spent casing is extracted from the chamber, and the casing is then ejected outward. After reaching the full extent of its rearward movement, the slide is then forced forward under spring pressure, stripping the next round from the magazine and inserting the round into the chamber. The firearm is then ready to fire again. It was all very simple. In a world which is so complex and often chaotic, the simplicity and predictability of firearms is a welcome change.

I also began to trust our two guides more. To come prepared as they did and to share these firearms with us demonstrated a certain level of faith in us, so I decided to reciprocate with an expression of gratitude.

"Arman," I said, "thank you for taking us to the mountains and helping us. Finding the Ark of Noah would mean a great deal to me and my son. You are truly a friend."

* * *

Arman and Yezras both smiled. "You are most welcome," Arman replied.

After more driving, I could see the approaching border check-point looming up ahead through the windshield. The checkpoint was small. One little hut was on the Azerbaijani side, populated by a lone border control official to check the passports of those leaving the country. A few yards away to the west was another little hut, this one on the Turkish side and likewise populated by a single official.

I wondered what would happen. Would our journey end here? Would we be turned back? Would we be arrested? Would we end up in the proverbial, yet all too real, Turkish prison like T.E. Lawrence?

Arman drove the car slowly up to the Azerbaijani check-point. The guard walked over to the driver's side window and peered in. He was dressed in a military uniform, with a holstered handgun on his right side and a rifle slung over his right shoulder. Arman and the guard began speaking to each other. I assumed it was in Azeri, as I didn't understand the language and thus couldn't follow the conversation. There was some discussion, pointing at us, and finally money exchanged hands - Arman handed a wad of bills to the guard who then waved us through. Shifting the car into gear, Arman drove across the border and stopped at the Turkish check-point where a nearly identical process ensued, except this time in Turkish. After Arman handed the requisite fee to the Turkish guard we were on our way.

"What happened?" asked Martin.

Yezras spoke, "They asked who we are and what we are doing. My father simply explained that we are going to see friends in Turkey, and we paid a small fee to leave Azerbaijan and enter into Turkey."

In many places one had to pay a "fee" for services; essentially a bribe couched in more opaque terms. The practice of paying bribes is prevalent throughout the world, but they are rarely called "bribes" outright. They tend to be termed in more innocuous phrasing as "fines" or "fees" which border guards and other officials require to be paid as additional padding on top of their meagre salaries. It was almost like a tip one would pay at a restaurant. This is the price of admission, I suppose. To the people here, it is treated as a necessary evil, something to be borne with and which, in the grand scheme of things, is simply a minor inconvenience if it means being able to go about one's life with minimal hassle from the government. It was just part of the cost of living here.

I owed Arman and his son another debt of gratitude for getting us successfully through the checkpoints and into Turkey. "Thank you, my friends," I said.

* * *

69

After another hour of driving in our cramped car, we finally arrived at the outskirts of the little town of Aralik. Lying at the extreme eastern corner of Turkey, the town was only about two miles from the Armenian border, and about sixteen miles from the peak of Greater Ararat. The entire area was sparsely populated; only 23,000 people live in the vicinity, with about 7,000 of those in the town itself. Most of the people are of Azeri or Kurdish descent. The "small town" in which I lived during my high school years was bigger.

The terrain around the town was nearly treeless, covered by mostly green grasses. The two main peaks of Ararat - capped by snow - loomed in the distance to the southwest, providing spectacular views for the townsfolk and for visitors like us. However, the geographical features seemed to be the physical manifestation of the foreboding I felt as I contemplated our ascent into that wilderness. Had I done the right thing in coming here? I had not only placed myself in danger, but my son as well. And now another man and his son had placed themselves into harm's way for my sake and for the sake of my quest. I would be saddened if any of them were injured or harmed on account of me.

Yet, I had come here seeking something, seeking the Ark. I had to keep going. In a strange way, though, it wasn't even as if it was too late to turn back. I could, of course, insist on going back right then and there. But, I couldn't seem to make that decision. It was as if I was on a course from which I could not deviate. There would be no quitting and no turning back, as some unseen force prohibited me from stopping and instead compelled me to continue on. I was propelled forward, almost reluctantly at this point, up to the saddle between the two mountain peaks to see what was there. Come fortune or evil, I would be there in short order.

"This is where we park." Arman broke my thoughts. Just outside the town of Aralik, he pulled the car off onto a gravel side road running perpendicular to the "highway" on which we were on and parked it in the grass next to a small, scraggly stand of trees.

We all poured out of the car and stretched. It felt good to stand, although I supposed I'd be doing a lot of that over the next few days. Perhaps I should have enjoyed the drive some more as well as the opportunity to sit.

Arman opened the trunk, and we retrieved our hiking gear, placing it on the ground while we prepared to depart.

"Do you think it is really up there, Mr. John," asked Yezras as he stared at the mountains in the distance.

"I don't know. I hope so. We shall find out soon enough, I suppose," I answered.

"If it is there, it has been hidden for a few

thousand years. Do you suppose that God wants anyone to find it? Perhaps He intends for it to remain hidden," continued Yezras.

Martin broke in, "Maybe over four thousand years. It's amazing to think that a ship the size which the Bible says it was could remain hidden, and in one piece, for that long."

Martin was right. The Bible says that the Ark was 300 cubits long, 50 cubits wide, and 30 cubits high. Assuming the cubit was 18 inches (there is some debate), that would mean the Ark was a huge ship: 450 feet long, 75 feet wide, and 45 feet high. Based on many estimates, it may have weighed nearly 8 million pounds and would have been capable of holding over 34 million pounds of cargo within its three decks. Certainly, that would allow it to contain a great many animals, as the Bible says it did. Indeed, it was the largest ship in the world until the Titanic; that ship didn't fare as well as the Ark did, however.

I thought for a moment. "I think the key phrase there is 'in one piece,' Martin. The Ark could very well have broken up over time, or rotted away, or carried away during millennia of snow, ice, storms, and earthquakes. Or, it may be on some other mountain far away from here. This may be a fool's errand on which we're embarking."

"Fools or not, we should get moving before it gets any later in the day," said Arman. "We should try to get to the foothills of the mountain before nightfall and then progress up the mountain tomorrow."

The foothills were about eight miles away. Most of this stretch of the hike would be across grassy plains. It was almost as if we were staring into the flatlands of Colorado, looking at the mountains rising above the ground in the distance. It was still hot now, but tomorrow as we climbed higher it would get much cooler, and more difficult.

CHAPTER TWELVE

Off On Foot

We grabbed our gear and prepared to set off for the mountains. I put on my lighter jacket for this stretch of the hike, leaving my heavy coat tied to my backpack. Yezras distributed the CZ 75s, along with 2 full magazines each. Upon receiving mine, I ejected the magazine, retracted the slide to ensure the chamber was clear, released the slide on an empty chamber, lowered the hammer, re-inserted the magazine, and then placed the weapon in my inner jacket pocket. Back home I would have carried a firearm such as this with a chambered round in a good holster, but here - with no holster - I preferred to carry it without a round in the chamber since the trigger was not protected from accidental discharge. If I actually needed to use the CZ, though, it would take a while to retrieve it from my jacket and then chamber a round. Another downside to not having a holster was the fact that the firearm weighed down the left side of my jacket; I zipped it at the bottom to help keep it from drooping too much.

With that done, I hoisted my pack onto my back and buckled its waist and chest straps. The others girded up with their packs as well. I turned to see Arman locking his car - why I couldn't fathom as there didn't seem to be anyone around, nor could I imagine who would stumble upon the car around here or take anything from it even if they did. Arman seemed pleased with himself, though, and put the keys in his pocket. After looking around one last time at our parking spot - although, it wasn't like we wouldn't remember where we left the car - we headed off to the south-west, with the imposing mountains looming ahead in the distance, separated from us by a few miles of grassy plains.

Thankfully, we had packed a few gallons of water. Water is heavy - about eight pounds per gallon - but it is a precious, life-sustaining commodity. The terrain we encountered after leaving the car confirmed what I had previously surmised from the maps and satellite images which I had consulted before we arrived: there was little water to be found in the area. We were approaching the mountain on the leeward side, so we had little hope of rain and there was no standing water. Nor would we likely be able to dig into the soil in order to trap condensation with the "plastic wrap trick" I had learned as a child; the ground was just too hard. Our success therefore depended on us reaching the snow deposits further up the mountain before we used up all our stores of water.

Even though the leeward side of the mountains

provided us with no water, there was an advantage to traveling to them from this direction. Since this flank of the peaks was drier, this meant that it was also less populated and we therefore had a lower chance of being seen or running into other people. The snow would provide ample water once we reached it; the water we toted with us in our packs sustaining us until then. We also had plenty of dried and preserved food. The human body can survive much longer without food than water, of course, but to be without food for too long on the mountain would likely be a death sentence, for we would be too weak to make it back off the mountain. Our cold, lifeless bodies would be added to the enduring mystique of the peaks.

Our planned stop tonight would be at the base of the mountains about eight miles away. That wasn't a bad hike at all, especially considering that the route there was relatively flat. After reaching a suitable spot, we would camp for the night, then continue the next day further up the slopes between the peaks of the mountains. We would make camp again before beginning the steeper ascent up the saddle which separated the peaks. We would spend an unknown number of days higher up on the saddle looking for the Ark. Each day we would have to identify a good camping spot by the early afternoon, since the weather tends to turn bad at the higher elevations around that time. We would wait out the foul weather during the evening, and then wake up early the next day to begin our search anew.

Our hope, then, was that once we finally made it to the saddle of the mountains we could make the best use of each day to have plenty of time to conduct our search for the Ark, or - more accurately - our search for the object which the locals reported they had seen from a distance. Our search area was huge, and we had only a general idea of where the reported object was, so we faced a rather formidable obstacle in actually locating it. The mountain itself would not assist us in this effort either. It would be cold, and there were many rocky crevices beyond which it would be impossible to see. I braced myself for the prospect of trudging across the rough slopes for many days, looking for something which we may never find. At some point we would be faced with the difficult decision of continuing the search or going home. I realized, though, that our food supplies would eventually help make that decision for us as they dwindled.

Onward we walked across the grassy landscape. The area nearest the town was surprisingly verdant, but further ahead I could tell that the landscape changed to a more somber brown. In just a few miles we would be at the threshold between green and brown, which seemed to symbolize the contrast between life and death. Was there death on this mountain? For us? For others who have engaged in the same quest?

We trudged along; we had to keep walking to make it to the foothills in time to make camp. Despite the uncertainty and difficulties which awaited us, I found time to admire the beautiful landscape and horizon, especially the blue sky above and the snow capped mountain ahead. I looked over at Martin and saw him regarding the countryside as well.

"It is beautiful country, isn't it?" I observed.

"Yes," answered Martin. "I was just wondering what it would have been like after the flood. Can you imagine the waters receding down off that mountain and Noah looking down onto this countryside?"

"And all the animals trekking down the mountain onto this plain," I continued the thought.

"Dad, how could so many animals fit on the Ark?" asked Martin.

"Well, it's a bit of a mystery, I suppose. But, consider that the animals may have been juveniles and that the Biblical concept of 'kind' may have meant those animals which could interbreed. My point is that Noah probably had to take many less types of animals than what we consider to be species. In fact, most of the variation in species probably arose after the flood as the various kinds of animals spread out onto the earth and adapted to their new habitats."

"You mean they evolved," said Martin.

* * *

"No, not exactly. I mean that as they bred in their new environments certain traits proved advantageous, leading to the wide diversity that we see. But, no new genetic information was added; the animals didn't become something they weren't before. Rather, they tended to self-select for survival, and the variations within the kinds - which we call species - developed in each type of habitat."

"Oh. You mean they just simply adapted to their environments."

"Yes," I answered.

"You Americans think too much." Arman broke into the conversation. "Why can you not let God's Word stand on its own? Why must you try to explain everything?"

"You make a valid point, I suppose," I responded back. Perhaps it was true that we try to rationalize everything. Could we not merely trust that what God says is true, without trying to prove that it is true? Was that not, in fact, why I was here - to prove that the flood is true by finding the Ark? I found in Arman's simple statement a searing rebuke. Had I placed myself, my son, and my two new friends in danger for the sake of "proving" something which didn't require proof?

After a few moments, Arman continued. "I used to work on a freighter in the Caspian sea. I can tell you that a ship of that size can carry a lot of cargo.

Nuh's ship was no different. It would have held a lot of animals, as the Lord's Holy Scriptures say. I do not need to see it to believe it." He paused. Grinning, he concluded, "However, it would be most wonderful to see it in person with my own eyes."

"Indeed it would," I said.

We continued onward. Arman explained that he and his family were actually of Armenian ethnic descent, not Azeri; he had been born in Nakhchivan to an Armenian family. The vast majority of the population of Azerbaijan was Muslim and of Azeri ethnicity, so Arman and his family were part of the minority in both religious and ethnic terms. There was an extremely small Christian community in Azerbaijan, most of whom were Armenian.

Pressing on with our hike, it occurred to me that it had been a long time since I had actually gone hiking. Martin and I had gone together over the years, and I had hiked and camped many times during my college years, but that was nearly twenty years ago. I was not the young man I was then. Now, my shoulders were getting sore and tired, and my feet and legs were beginning to feel the burden of my pack and its contents. I hoped that I could make the ascent up the mountain. It had only been a short time since we left the car and I was already beginning to get tired.

I had little time to bemoan my condition, though. Suddenly, our peaceful walk was interrupted.

The Mountains of Ararat

CHAPTER THIRTEEN

The Encounter

I heard a noise to my left. What I saw next sent my heart racing. A group of men armed with rifles began running towards us. They had appeared from behind a small rock formation and looked to be carrying AK-47s, which were ubiquitous in this part of the world. They ran towards us as I felt my jacket to double-check that I still had the CZ 75 in my pocket. I hoped to avoid a gunfight, though, since our little band, armed only with handguns and taken completely by surprise, had little chance against a dozen armed men with rifles.

As they approached, they began yelling and motioning. They seemed to want us to lie down. This was no good, I thought; no good comes from lying down in front of armed men. I did not see that we had a choice at this point, though. There was no chance of fighting back right now; we were at a severe disadvantage both on account of numbers as well as position. My hope lie in either de-escalating the situation, or staying alive long enough to find an opportune moment to make a move which would hopefully save us.

As we all dropped to the earth with our arms outstretched, Arman began speaking to the armed men. I could not understand what they were saying, of course. However, they were yelling back and forth to each other. By this point all four of us were on the ground, with the armed men directly in front of us with rifles at the ready. We were roughly in a line; I was on the extreme left, Martin to my immediate right, then Arman, and finally Yezras on the extreme right of our little group. We were all face-down. Arman was still speaking with the men, and they seemed to be arguing. I wondered if this would be my last memory and my last moment on earth. How would my wife learn of my death? Would she blame me for causing the death of Martin as well? I certainly felt guilty at putting him in this situation. If we all died, his death - as well as the deaths of Arman and Yezras - would be my fault. I was filled with despair and sorrow at the thought.

Finally, Arman spoke English to Martin and I, "They say that we are trespassing on the holy mountain and will take us back to their village. What they will do then is unknown."

These must be the locals whom Arman had warned us about. To be moved to another location by them was a bad development, I thought. I knew that with common criminals, the moment they moved their victims to another location the odds of their victims surviving the encounter dropped greatly. Generally, assailants moved their victims in order to kill them. This was not a comforting thought in our present situation. My heart sank further. I was most concerned about Martin's safety. I had lived a good life so far and was prepared to meet my Creator, even if - given the choice - I would prefer to delay the meeting. Martin, however, was still a young man. He still had a long life ahead of him. Weighing further on my conscience was the fact that Arman and Yezras should not even be here.

Before I could continue following this chain of thought, we were all jerked to our feet by one of the men and then shoved forward as he screamed something at us. I could feel the muzzle of a rifle poking my side. Now we had armed men all around us, front and back and both sides as they formed us into a column to march us to their village.

"He says to walk," explained Arman.

Walk we did. I saw little alternative at the moment.

"Arman, is there a way to get us out of this?"

As soon as I said this, I felt a sharp knock on the back of my head and everything went black.

CHAPTER FOURTEEN

Awakening

Where was I? As I woke up and sought to rouse myself, I instinctively leaned over on my left side to turn off my alarm clock, but I couldn't find it. Slowly, I opened my eyes and began to fitfully look around the room. It was then that I realized that I did not recognize any of my surroundings and that I was not at home. I had experienced this feeling many times before when I used to travel frequently for work. Often when traveling I would wake up in the hotel the next morning and not realize or remember where I was at first; it took a few seconds to make sense of the new environs. One's mind grows used to waking up at home, and when not at home is at first confused upon waking from sleep in a hotel.

I was having the same feeling now, although this was obviously no hotel. It was a small, dank room in which I seemed to have found myself. I was lying on a dirt floor. The walls were wooden, with cobwebs and darkness pervading the space. The memories came back to me of what had led me to this place. I remembered the gunmen we had encountered on our hike towards the mountains. The last thing I could remember was being forced to walk at gunpoint by them. Now I'm here. Where are the others? I looked around. There was no Martin, Arman, or Yezras. Oh, God, I hope Martin is ok. I hope they all are.

Fear and sadness began to overtake me. I thought of my wife. Would I ever see her again? Would I die here in some strange place, never seeing my wife or son again? Would I experience my last moments on earth in this foreign land, preceded possibly by the intense pain and suffering of torture? Would my wife even know what had happened? Would Martin and I just be "disappeared?" Our family back home may wonder for the rest of their own lives what had become of us. They may just assume that we had died on the mountain. Would they come looking for us?

I had come here looking for something myself. I was seeking something. Ostensibly it was the Ark of Noah. But was that all? Had I come searching for more than that? Proof of the truth of the Scriptures, of God's revelation of Himself to us? A piece of myself even, to prove that I had a purpose in life by finding something which had served the greatest purpose? Was it just to prove that I still had the strength and vigor to battle the heights of the mountains and the resultant elements? Whatever the real reason I had come so far, was it worth it now?

A man walked into the room. There was so little light that I could barely see his face. However, I could make out that he was carrying a knife. What little light was available in the room reflected off the steel blade. At that moment I realized I was bound. My hands and feet were tied in ropes, preventing any movement on my part; I was completely helpless.

"Your name is John Welz? American?"

I was taken aback that the man spoke English and knew my name. He must have looked through my pockets and found my passport. Before I could answer, he knelt down next to me. I could see his face more clearly now. It was round with pockmarks on the portions of his skin which were not covered by his graying beard. His demeanor was rough and direct.

"John Welz?" he asked again as he tapped me on the arm.

Finally I answered, "Yes, that is my name, and, yes, my son Martin and I are Americans. Is he ok? Are the others ok?"

"What are you doing here?"

My mind raced on how best to answer this question. Should I make up a lie, or tell the truth about our purposes here? I wasn't sure how much this man already knew, or what would best serve my interests in this situation. After some thought, I decided that there was a very good chance that he had already talked with the others, so I felt it was not worth the risk of lying. I would tell him the truth, and pray for the best.

"We are on our way to the mountains of Ararat to look for the Ark of Noah," I said.

"I know."

Although taken aback at his response, I was glad now that I had not lied. He must have talked to the others already; hopefully, I thought, just "talked to" and not "interrogated" was the correct word. I prayed that the others were safe.

The man continued, "When we saw your group, we assumed you were Turks, which is why we intercepted you and picked you up."

I was confused, "Turks?"

"Yes," he said as he cut the ropes which bound me, freeing my hands and feet. He helped me sit up and sat down next to me. I rubbed my wrists and ankles, which had been chaffed by the fibers of the ropes.

"We are Kurds, fighting for our own homeland. We fight Daesh - the Islamic State as you may know it - in Iraq and Syria, and the Turks here. Our hope is to win our freedom and gain the ability to govern ourselves in our own homeland. My name is Bakur. Your son and friends are ok."

I wondered at this man who had so quickly captured us when he thought we were Turks, but who just as quickly was releasing us once he realized we were not.

"Why do you fight the Turks?" I wondered.

"Our people live throughout the region. In Turkey, Iraq, Syria, Iran, and Armenia. We are the descendants of the ancient Medes and have lived here for thousands of years, but have watched our lands ruled by successive groups of foreigners. Our aim is to unite together the Kurds who live across these lands and finally rule ourselves, without interference from anyone else. I believe your country had a similar goal once?"

"Yes," I said. "We became independent from Great Britain over two centuries ago."

"We seek something similar," he said deliberately. He seemed thoughtful in his response, and I felt a strange sense of good-will towards him, even though he had mistreated me at our first meeting. The longing for freedom and liberty is embedded deep within the human conscience. I feel it, and this man here feels it as well. Despite our other differences, I could meet him at the intersection of our mutual desire for liberty.

* * *

"I wish you and your people the best. I know that you have been one of the few to successfully fight the Islamic State and am familiar with your struggle for your homeland.   You are a strong and proud people."

"Thank you," he said. Then, he continued, "Your friends are safe, as is your son. They are eating in the other building in our encampment here. You were the last we have spoken with because you have been asleep for quite some time... from hitting your head."   This was certainly quit a passive way of referring to the fact that his men had hit me on the back of the head with a rifle to knock me unconscious. "Let me take you to them. You will eat and rest, then tomorrow we will drive you in our trucks to the base of the mountains to which you were headed. It will save you many miles of walking. You will need all your energy for the mountain; it is a brutal master. I wish you the best in your struggle, for it will certainly be great."   As he said this he laughed, slapped me on the back, and then led me out of the room into the daylight outside.

As I emerged from the room, my eyes shuttered at the brightness of the sun as they sought to adjust from the darkness to which they had become accustomed. The shock at seeing the light and the bruise on the back of my head made me wince. I tried to adjust to my surroundings as I looked around. I could see that the building in which I had been kept in was one of many. Bakur led me across a small grassy field to another, larger building. Entering, I saw Martin, Arman, and Yezras. They ran to me and inquired how I was.

"I am fine, just hungry. And, I have a splitting headache."

We sat down together at a small wooden table where they had been eating their meal. I noticed that Bakur's men were eating together at a larger table nearby; they were wearing camouflage uniforms. A woman came over to our table and brought me a plate of meat and bread, along with a glass of water. She was also wearing a uniform and armed with a rifle. Nearby, there was another table of women, similarly attired. Everyone here seemed to be a fighter of some sort. The Kurds were truly a nation of people willing to fight for their independence. I was happy for the hot meal and dug right in, starving as I was. I was also hoping that the food would help my headache.

"I am glad we are all ok," said Martin. "I guess we're spending the night here?"

"Yes, I think so," I said. "Bakur said they would take us to the base of the mountain in the morning."

"It is good providence that we ran into Kurds, rather than Turks," observed Arman. "The Turks would likely have detained us and sent us home. The Kurds at least are friendly towards us, not so much towards the Turks, though. "

* * *

"I have perceived that," I said.

We ate our meals and then drank the goat's milk which was offered to us as a sort of dessert. After we were done, Bakur led us to a small hut which was to be our lodgings for the night. He bid us good night and then headed to his own hut. Our little space was a tight fit for four people, but the sleeping cots inside managed to fit around the perimeter of the hut, with a small open area in the center.

As we entered, we each claimed a cot and placed our belongings alongside. I took off my jacket and then changed into my sleeping clothes - a pair of sweatpants and insulated socks I had brought along for the purpose. Everything else went into my pack.

"Shall we pray?" asked Yezras.

Pray. It had completely slipped from my mind to do so while on this journey. I had been so caught up in the frenetic activity of getting here to the cusp of the mountain that I had forgotten all about prayer. Strangely, searching for Noah's Ark had caused me to nearly forget about God Himself. I had become so preoccupied with the creation that I had forgotten the Creator Himself. Perhaps that is why the Ark has been hidden for so long? Does the search for religious truth cause one to actually fall away from God? Is it such that a person's focus begins to shift away from God and towards the object instead?

I wondered if this also applied to the Scriptures themselves. Was the search for the Ark emblematic of something more? Is it possible to dive too deep into the text of the Scriptures and thereby forget just from whom they come? Do we end up losing the greater story of God's salvation of us through Christ the more we pick apart the grammar and vocabulary of the Bible? Is it possible that we lose the forest by staring too much at the trees, so to speak? Certainly, I knew many people who knew the Scriptures quite well, but who nonetheless lacked faith. I also knew people who could quote certain portions very well, but who did not understand the larger story. It is always good to read the Bible, but it is necessary to keep the larger narrative in mind. The Biblical narrative is centered around the Holy Lord God's salvation of sinful humanity by His grace on account of Jesus Christ. The Scriptures serve the purpose of telling this story, of revealing God's actions and plans for us. Reading the Bible without understanding or appreciating this larger picture causes one to miss the whole point of the Scriptures and thus how they are centered on Christ.

My thoughts drifted back more concretely to the Ark itself. If it were found, would it actually have a different effect than the one I for which I had hoped? I trusted that finding it would cause more people to come to faith. However, could the opposite actually happen? Is it the case that finding the Ark would remove it from being an article of faith, placing it instead into the realm of fact, and once a fact as something which would be debated and discounted by those without faith, leaving no one closer to God than before? I had begun this search thinking that finding the Ark, showing the world that it exists, would somehow prove the existence of God and what He has done throughout history. Yet now, within the synecdoche of my own life, I saw that perhaps this was a futile hope. Even as I had forgotten about God in the quest for the object which is one of the most prominent in the history of His relation to the world, so too would others forget about God, and still fail to honor Him, if the object were found. They would focus on the object and forget about the One who had used it for His purposes, seeing only the trees and missing the forest.

Disheartened, I answered Yezras, "Yes, we should most certainly pray."

We then all prayed together to our God: two Americans joining with two Armenians - fathers and sons - in the land of the Turks, guarded by Kurds. The world is truly a strange and small place, I thought. As we gave thanks to our God for guiding us safely thus far and implored Him for continued protection up the slopes, it occurred to me that here in this time and place the true meaning of Christ's Church achieved tangible form. Separated by culture, nationality, and native language, the four of us were nevertheless united in Christ and part of His Church. My thoughts soared to the past, considering those of the Church who had gone before us, those I have not yet met, but would someday meet in person at the promised resurrection of the body and the life everlasting, as the Creed holds. The thought came to me that the Christian hope of the resurrection is actually the hope of a re-union of sorts. It is the hope and promise to finally meet in person those who are also part of this family of faith, along with our God as well. This is the true Christian hope, not finding an object connected with God. For one day all our hopes will be fulfilled and our faith completed, and that day was coming. I got a glimpse of that day now as the four of us prayed together, the day when the whole Church would be united in person. I saw a glimmer of the future, and it was beautiful.

We closed our prayer saying together, "In the name of Jesus Christ our Lord and Savior, Amen."

Amen indeed.

CHAPTER FIFTEEN

To The Camp

I woke up to the sound of someone yelling into our hut to wake us up. I really didn't want to get up yet; I could have slept for a few more hours. I looked up to see who was waking us. It was Bakur. He was standing at the rickety door of our lodgings, urging us out of our sleep to begin the day. As he left, I could see that the sky was just beginning to lighten; soon the sun would be completely up. It was chillier this morning than on the previous mornings we had spent in Nakhchivan. It would turn colder once we finally made our way to the base of the mountains.

The others in the hut began to rise also. Martin, Arman, and Yezras all - in their own ways - shuffling off the coils of sleep. Last night we had all prayed together as Christians, and I felt a special bond with them on that basis as our small portion of the Church communed together as one. Now I observed the common human bond which we all shared as well: the need for sleep and the difficulty with rising from it. Sleep captures all of us, regardless of our background or nationality. Death, the ultimate sleep, eventually subdues us as well. Sleep and death are among the things we all have in common, in addition to the natural cycles of the body, the desire to love and be loved, the need to have some hope to head towards. I realized that these were all things which we shared together as people, even if some abused or misused these common needs. The four of us, and our Kurdish host, were united in our essential humanity.

I also reflected upon that word which we as Americans like to use, even as we decry separation based upon it: race. We talk much of race, but in the Bible there is no concept of race in the sense that we use it. God created humanity, and we are all descended from the same two original parents: Adam and Eve. Thus, all humanity comes from the same two people, and we are all related to each other. There are therefore not separate "races" of humans; this idea of "race" sprang from evolutionary theories which postulated that various races of humans arose from different parts of the world under the pressure of natural selection which lead to divergent traits differentiating the races.

This false belief led, in the 20th century, to horrifying notions such as eugenics and the corresponding pursuit of achieving "racial" perfection. The Nazis and many others experimented on humans in an effort to purge the human genome of traits or characteristics which they considered less than ideal so as to achieve "racial" purity. All of this, however, is counter to God's design and plan; it is yet another way in which man tries to "play god" while refusing to accept the truth of God's creation. There is only one race; the color or shade of one's skin does not make a person somehow qualitatively different from a person with a different color or shade of skin. Racial distinctions were invented by fallen humans as yet another way to divide people from one another. It is an effort to deny the essential humanity of those who look, talk, or act different from us.

In this foreign land, I began to realize the truth of all this. It came home to me that we are all basically the same as people. It also occurred to me that rather than talking about "race," the Bible makes a distinction concerning the "nations." The Greek word for nation is "ethnos;" it is from where we get the word "ethnicity." A "nation" in the Biblical context is a group of people who share a common language and culture. The nations were created after the dispersion at Babel, when God confused the languages of the people, forcing them to spread throughout the earth; the various nations arose from this event. God did this in order to force them to carry out the commission He had given to them to fill the earth. The nations were a visible manifestation of the diversity of God's human creations.

Even though God separated humanity at Babel, though, He promised to eventually gather all nations together around the Christ, the Savior of all nations.

Throughout the Old Testament, in many places, God promised that the nations would come to God's Holy Mountain, and the New Testament makes this promise more clear once Christ arrives. For it is Christ who is the one to whom the nations come and in whom all nations are united.

I got a glimpse of this last night as two Americans and two Armenians prayed together to Christ our Lord. It was a small foreshadowing of what God has in store for us at the resurrection when we are all united together in person. I reflected upon the vision of the coming resurrection which was given to St. John (Revelation 7-10):

After this I looked, and behold, a great multitude that no one could number, from every nation, from all tribes and peoples and languages, standing before the throne and before the Lamb, clothed in white robes, with palm branches in their hands, and crying out with a loud voice, 'Salvation belongs to our God who sits on the throne, and to the Lamb!

It came home to me that God's desire is that all people receive this salvation through Christ. We truly are all related, but separated due to the sin of Adam and Eve. Yet, God is gathering us together as His Church united in Christ. Here in this strange land, among these strange people, I began to see this more clearly. The budding friendship of Martin and I with Arman and Yezras was but a microcosm of the Church as a whole and what God has in store for her when Christ returns. God is bringing the nations together around Christ, and I saw a small image of that here with our two Armenian friends.

I had allowed my thoughts to carry me away from the present moment. Martin came to my side next to my cot, "Dad, we need to get up so we can get on the road soon."

Everyone else, I now noticed, was already up and getting dressed for the day. Finally, I rose also and began to get ready. I dressed and packed my gear, then headed with the others over to breakfast which consisted of some eggs, cheese, and tomatoes. I could almost forget that I was in Turkey and think instead that I was in England; the Kurds and the English seemed to be culinary cousins (I'm not sure this is necessarily complementary towards the Kurds). The food was good, though, especially since I knew that I should enjoy the hot meal while I had the opportunity. I also greatly appreciated their hospitality and thanked them for it.

Following breakfast, we loaded ourselves and our gear into the bed of a four-wheel-drive pickup truck and headed off towards the mountains. Bakur drove us, and one of his soldiers manned the passenger seat in the cab. It wasn't quite the "shotgun seat;" more like the "rifle seat," based on his weapon of choice. After about an hour we arrived at the base of the mountains. The plan was to camp here for the rest of the day and night and then begin our ascent on the following morning. We wanted to have the chance to further acclimate ourselves to the rising elevation before embarking up the mountain.

It seemed like a wasted day, but we planned to make the most of it by exploring a bit around the surrounding area.

We leapt from the truck and then unloaded all our gear, placing it in a pile a few feet away. Bakur had returned to us all our belongings, including our CZ 75s. I again stashed mine back inside my inner jacket pocket, being sure to ensure the chamber was clear. I did notice, though, that Bakur - professional soldier that he was - made sure to clear the weapon and lock back the slide before handing it to me. I was appreciative of the proper hand-off and nodded knowingly to him. Upon receiving it, I made sure to clear it in front of him to acknowledge the safe transfer of the weapon.

After making sure we had all our things, Bakur turned to us before leaving, shook our hands heartily, and said, "I wish you much good fortune and peace. May you find what it is you seek."

"And you as well," I said.

Then, we parted ways from our Kurdish escort. They headed back to their camp and their struggle, while we prepared for ours.

CHAPTER SIXTEEN

Base Camp

After Bakur drove off, we looked for a suitable spot to make camp within the general vicinity of where he had dropped us off. We decided to ascend slightly higher, towards a level spot we had glimpsed a few hundred yards distant on the slopes. Thus, we collected our gear from where we had deposited it and headed to the location we had identified. It only took us about half an hour to reach it, at which point we dropped our gear and began to make camp.

We had brought two tents with us. Martin and I would sleep in one, while Arman and Yezras would sleep in the other. We pitched the tents such that they were on either side of a common fire pit. Driving the tent stakes into the ground was difficult, but we managed it; some, however, we had to place very shallow due to the rocky ground. For the fire pit we dug a few inches into the rough soil and then made a circle of rocks around the pit. On top of the pit we placed a folding metal rack which we had brought for cooking. We could place our pots and pans on the rack to heat our meals.

After preparing our camp, we decided to go look around the area together. It was still fairly early in the day, so we had plenty of time before nightfall. There were no trees in sight, simply small grasses and rock. The sun beat down on us, but the air was nice and cool. We were on the north-eastern base of the mountains, with the larger peak of Ararat to our south-west, and the smaller peak nearly directly to our south. We were currently at an elevation of just over four thousand feet above sea level. The peaks, of course, were much higher, with Greater Ararat rising to nearly seventeen thousand feet and Lesser Ararat almost thirteen thousand feet above sea level. The ground in this area rolled gently upwards until becoming much steeper in the distance. Our intended destination was the saddle between the two peaks. We would not attempt to reach it until tomorrow, however.

For now we contented ourselves with exploring the more immediate area around our camp. We headed to the south across the rolling slopes. After a few minutes of walking we found a large depression in the earth. It must have been nearly two hundred feet long and about a hundred feet wide, sunken into the earth at a depth of fifty feet. The ground in and around the depression was punctuated by rocky striations. I had seen pictures of similar geological formations which litter this area. Over the years some of these had actually been reported as the Ark, until further investigation revealed that they were composed of merely stone. Seeing one of them in person, I could now understand how a person could mistake it for a boat. This particular formation approximated the relative dimensions and shape of a large boat; it was, however, just rock. I hoped that what the locals had seen up on the saddle of the mountains, and to which we were ultimately heading, was not just another rock formation. The Ark has been claimed to have been found many times previously, but in each case all that people had "found" were simply these strange-looking, natural formations.

We looked around the formation, exploring the perimeter. I took a number of pictures to document the find. Then, we descended down to the bottom of the depression. The sides were like steep, craggy cliffs; the bottom was fairly uniform and filled with grass and small rocks. We spent some time down there looking around. Afterwards, as we ascended back up the sides I admired the beauty of the landscape and spotted additional formations such as this one located further up on the slopes of the mountain. I noted that the formations seemed to flow down from the mountain peaks, perpendicular to the peaks and parallel to one another. It occurred to me that they looked like erosion patterns. I imagined flood waters receding from the peaks four thousand years ago and eroding away the looser soil, leaving the rocky striations and the inner depressions to remain.

The two peaks of the mountains were in the

distance. Our present position was about five miles from the larger peak and seven miles from the smaller peak. Our target was the mid-point of the saddle between the two peaks, lying a few miles distant. Of course, the actual walking distance would be longer, due to the elevation change and the necessity of making switchbacks during the climb. I pulled out my binoculars to get a better look at our destination. The peaks and the approaches up the saddle were covered in snow, as were the higher portions all around the mountains as well. The nearer part of the mountains closer to us was clear of snow, however. Peering up at the slopes of the saddle, I could not detect what the locals had reported they had glimpsed after the earthquake. There was, as of yet, no Ark to be seen.

After our little expedition, we returned to camp and reorganized our packs for the coming ascent in the morning. Within my and Martin's tent, I laid out fresh socks for the morning and re-filled my canteens with water from the larger containers we had brought with us. I also got my out my thicker coat from my pack and stored snacks such as beef jerky and protein bars in its front pockets; I put my CZ 75 within the inner pocket. I tested my flashlight, placing it in a coat pocket as well. My camera still had plenty of battery life, although I had brought a spare, and a huge amount of space was available on the SD card for pictures. I organized my topographic maps within my map carrier, making sure to mark our present position on the appropriate map with a red grease pencil.

Afterwards, there was still time remaining before nightfall, so I grabbed my Bible and went off a short distance to read alone. I found a large rock to lean against and began to read Genesis 6:

Now the earth was corrupt in God's sight, and the earth was filled with violence. And God saw the earth, and behold, it was corrupt, for all flesh had corrupted their way on the earth.

And God said to Noah, "I have determined to make an end of all flesh, for the earth is filled with violence through them. Behold, I will destroy them with the earth. Make yourself an ark of gopher wood. Make rooms in the ark, and cover it inside and out with pitch.

This is how you are to make it: the length of the ark 300 cubits, its breadth 50 cubits, and its height 30 cubits. Make a roof for the ark, and finish it to a cubit above, and set the door of the ark in its side. Make it with lower, second, and third decks.

For behold, I will bring a flood of waters upon the earth to destroy all flesh in which is the breath of life under heaven. Everything that is on the earth shall die.

But I will establish my covenant with you, and you shall come into the ark, you, your sons, your wife, and your sons' wives with you. And of every living thing of all flesh, you shall bring two of every sort into the ark to keep them alive with you. They shall be male and female. Of the birds according to their kinds, and of the animals according to their kinds, of every creeping thing of the ground, according to its kind, two of every sort shall come in to you to keep them alive. Also take with you every sort of food that is eaten, and store it up. It shall serve as food for you and for them."

Noah did this; he did all that God commanded him.

The flood was a very visible and powerful demonstration of both God's righteous judgement against sin as well as His mercy towards His creation. He had destroyed the world with the waters, yet saved Noah and his family as well as animal life. The instrument of their salvation was the Ark which God had instructed Noah to build. It is for this reason that Christians throughout the centuries have looked upon Noah's Ark as a representation or image of the Church herself. Through the Church, God saves us as well as preserves life on earth for the sake of His Church. The physical Ark has long been lost, but the spiritual ark of the Church lives on.

Now, however, we were here on these mountains seeking to find this physical Ark of Noah. I wondered if we would find it, or if we would just encounter another boat-shaped rock formation like the one we had explored earlier. Was this just a futile quest? Or, if we actually did manage to find the Ark, would it meet my expectations for the size and significance of the find? What would finding the Ark mean for the Church and for non-believers? Would it have any effect, change any minds, strengthen anyone's faith? These thoughts swirled through my head as I continued to read the Genesis account of the flood and its aftermath.

After reading for a while longer, I noticed that the sun had begun to get low in the horizon, so I returned to camp. The others had started to prepare dinner. They had a nice fire going in the pit and had the metal rack set up over the flames. Upon my return, Arman retrieved some preserved lamb meat which he had brought with him, and we cooked it on the fire. We all sat in a circle around the blaze. Arman had also packed a couple loaves of homemade bread, so he distributed pieces of one of the loaves amongst us as well. I had a bottle of wine which I had carefully nursed during our travels thus far and which - amazingly - was still unscathed. I figured that we might as well drink it now, since I wasn't sure if I'd be able to protect it and keep it unbroken during the hike tomorrow and the next few days. Opening the bottle, I passed it around the cooking fire, and we all drank as we ate our dinner. It was probably the best camping dinner I had ever had.

As we ate, we shared stories about our lives and grew to know one another better. This was the purpose of meals, really - to commune with one another and form bonds of friendship. It was the reason business has traditionally been conducted over meals, why families eat together, why Jesus himself shared meals with his disciples and those whom he wished to teach. Indeed, the Church celebrates Communion - the Lord's Supper - believing that it is with the bread and wine that the

Lord Himself dwells with us. As physical creatures, we take comfort and solace in food and find friendship in the shared experience of a meal.

We all learned more about each other during this meal. Arman explained that he had spent his youth working as a shepherd near Nakhchivan. One of his early enjoyments in life was making trips into Turkey to hike near the mountains. This is when he first became familiar with the stories of the local shepherds concerning the Ark on the mountain. Some of the old timers in the area had claimed to have seen the Ark during exceptionally warm years when the snows melted at the higher elevations. Arman had never seen it, though; it was simply legend to him. Later, when he got older, he took a job as a merchant marine, hauling cargo around the Caspian Sea in his desire to see more of the world. However, once he met his wife he decided to pursue a more settled existence and moved back to Nakhchivan where they started a family together. In turn, I told of my upbringing and travels as well as how I met my wife in college. She and I also settled down together to start a family and begin careers. Arman and I continued to trade stories about married life as we laughed together at the universal humorous moments in a marriage.

The two boys, Martin and Yezras, spoke of their own plans for the future. They were still young men at the cusp of their lives, while Arman and I were older and getting ready to hand the reigns off to this next generation. Martin was currently in college, studying to be an engineer. He wanted to be a civil engineer and build roads, bridges, and grand structures. Yezras was working small jobs in his hometown, trying to save money so he could afford to go off to college. He wanted to be a software developer and was already self-taught enough to have created a variety of games and applications, making some money through these means as well. The boys also talked about girls and their hopes for having their own wives and families some day. It truly is a small world, I thought. Our lives, hopes, and desires are not so different from one another. At heart, we wanted to live peaceful lives with our families in homes filled with love and have something interesting to put our talents toward.

After finishing our meals and discussions, we rose and began to clean up the eating and cooking area. Arman tossed some dirt on the remaining flames of the fire to extinguish them. I collected the refuse from our meal, enclosing it in a sealed plastic bag. We could not afford to take the trash with us up the mountain, so I buried it in a shallow hole. Upon our descent from the mountains, we planned to encamp at this spot again where I would retrieve our trash and the other items we would leave here, such as our surplus clothing which was suitable only for warmer weather. Hopefully everything would still be here when we returned.

After finishing the policing of the area, we all prayed together and then wished each other a good night.

"Tomorrow will be an exciting day," observed Martin.

"Yes," I agreed. "I am glad that we will finally be starting the main part of our expedition. I'm looking forward to getting further up on the mountains."

"We must wake and leave camp early so that we have more daylight to look for the Ark of Nuh," said Arman.

We all nodded in agreement. Then, we headed to our respective tents, as father-son teams, to rest until the morning.

CHAPTER SEVENTEEN

Night Thoughts

Martin and I crawled into our tent to prepare for sleep. Our two sleeping bags were oriented side-by-side, with the entrance of the tent at our feet. Before entering my bag, I first changed into a separate set of clothes for sleeping and removed my socks in an attempt to keep my hiking clothes as dry as possible. When camping outdoors, clothing tends to get damp from sweat and dew, so I wished to protect my clothing from these as much as I possibly could while I slept. From past experience as well, I knew that dry feet were important both physically and psychologically; I had packed a stash of socks in sealed baggies for this expedition. I placed my boots inside the tent at the foot of my sleeping bag and my hiking clothes in a drawstring bag nearby. In the morning, during breakfast, my plan was to dry them of any accumulated dew by laying them near the fire as we cooked. Our two backpacks we crammed into a the limited space remaining near our heads.

In my younger days I rarely used a tent. Instead, I

would sleep in a small, mesh hammock strung between two trees. In a strange way, I had always felt safer this way; I could more easily see my surroundings and inspect any strange noises during the night. Of course, it would be impossible to camp in this way here; there were no large trees where we were, and the weather was not inviting for sleeping without cover. I was also, of course, older and less willing to subject myself to physical hardships if they were avoidable. When I was a younger man I took a perverse pride in enduring discomfort, to prove to myself how tough I was. Now, though, I had learned to enjoy comfort when it was available. The available comfort on this present adventure would certainly be sparse. The ground was hard and the weather was turning colder. Tomorrow would be a long day of hiking as well, taking its toll on my feet and back.

As I lay in my sleeping bag, I had trouble falling asleep. I was both excited and anxious. I was excited due to the potential of finding the long-lost Ark. To locate such an incredibly important and historic artifact roused my imagination. I felt like a child on Christmas Eve, eagerly anticipating what the next day would bring. I could barely relax long enough to fall asleep. My mind was racing; thinking about finding the Ark was mind-boggling and various possibilities swirled through my mind. Did the Ark even exist? If it did, it is still up here on this mountain? What would it look like if we actually found it? Could we find it?

* * *

I was anxious as well, though, because I knew that the trek up the mountains to look for the Ark would be dangerous. The weather would turn colder, and the rocky terrain would become harder to traverse. We had enough supplies to last us about a week and a half on the mountain, assuming we carefully rationed our food and melted snow for water. If we were fortunate and found the Ark sooner, we would be able to sustain ourselves much better through increased calorie intake. However, we would start with smaller rations, just in case our trek lasted longer than we desired. The earlier meal we enjoyed this evening would be our last "big" meal for a while. The rest of our time on the mountain would bring nothing but hunger and fatigue.

The thought of Martin also weighed on my mind. I hoped that I did not make a mistake in bringing him along on this search. In reality, I was actually of two minds concerning this. On the one hand, I was happy to share this experience with my son. Whether we found the Ark or not, it would be a life-changing trip for both of us. On the other hand, though, I regretted the fact that I had endangered his safety, first in the previous encounter with the Kurds and soon in the coming encounter with the mountain. The trail which lay before us would be a difficult one.

I also thought of my wife. I missed her deeply. She had supported my desire in coming here. In fact, she had been more than just supportive; she had urged me on, encouraging me to pursue the opportunity of a lifetime and seek what I was looking for. Through the separation induced by this trip, though, I began to realize that I had already received from God all that I needed. Before coming here on this expedition, I had thought that I needed to find the Ark in order to somehow be complete or to fulfill my calling or vocation, but now it started to occur to me that this was not so. Finding the Ark was not necessary for me to be whole. I already had all that I needed: a wife, a son, a daughter, and the opportunity to enjoy life with them. My life was complete with them, and I had ample opportunity to fulfill my vocation as a husband and father with them. However, I had endangered all of this in coming here. Was I being selfish? Had I acted rashly in leaving what I had in order to seek out something more?

My home lay thousands of miles away, but in some sense it was also with me. From my previous travels, I knew that there was always a piece of my home which I carried with me in my heart, no matter where I was. Now, at the base of this strange mountain, on the cusp of beginning a great quest, I again felt the flames of my home within me. Memories came rushing back to me. The soft skin of my wife, the warm embrace of her arms, the times we rested together on our couch or on our hammock in the yard. The taste of the food we enjoyed together, the red wine, the cocktails on special occasions. Working in the yard together, buying furniture for our house over the years, the drive to church on Sunday mornings, raising our children together. All these shared moments came back to me, as if my life were in review before my mind's eye.

It was hard to be away from home, away from all these comforts and joys which had flooded my thoughts. Yet, I had temporarily left all these behind to come here for a purpose. Would I find what I was seeking? Would I find something more?

Then, with these thoughts resting upon my heart and soul, I drifted off to sleep.

CHAPTER EIGHTEEN

Breaking Camp

I woke before sunrise. The cool mountain air invaded the tent, singeing my face with its bite. I wanted to crawl deeper into my sleeping bag to attempt to warm myself, but I knew that I must rise so that we could begin our trek further up the mountain as soon as possible. We had a lot to accomplish today. With reluctance, then, I emerged from my sleeping bag and grabbed my clothing from the bag at my feet, intending to bring it outside to the fire pit to dry it from the residual dew which had accumulated. I put on my boots and the previous day's pair of socks in order to go outside, intending to switch to a fresh pair of socks later, after I warmed my boots by the fire. Martin awoke as I was getting ready and did much the same. Emerging from our tent and dragging our packs with us, we saw Arman and Yezras. It appeared that they had just gotten up as well and had begun preparing the fire pit for breakfast.

We exchanged "good mornings" and inquired into

how each party had slept. We all agreed that it was a decent night, considering the circumstances of our lodgings - sleeping on hard ground in the cold wilderness. Martin and I staggered over to the fire pit, placing our clothing on rocks next to it to begin the drying out process. We then set to work with assisting the other two with cooking breakfast. I retrieved some canned beans from my pack, and Arman produced some salted ham from his. For the beans, I simply opened the lid and then heated them directly in the can. The ham we placed on the metal rack to heat up. I was dying for a cup of coffee, so I warmed some water in a metal pot and then mixed in some instant coffee. We had all brought utensils, cups, plates, and bowls in our separate packs, so after breakfast was ready, we shared everything amongst ourselves. It was a suitably fine breakfast for such a location and good fuel for what was likely going to be a long day.

As we drank our instant coffee after eating, we talked about the day ahead.

"I suppose today that we simply head uphill?" asked Arman.

"I guess so," I answered. "We'll start heading up the slopes towards the saddle to see what we can see."

"It will get colder today as we go up."

I thought for a moment. "Yes, I think maybe we'll

keep going until it gets later in the day and then we'll look for a good location to camp further up the mountain. Then, the next morning we can start out again in our search for the Ark."

Arman agreed, "Yes, that should help shelter us from the poor weather which will blanket the mountains by late afternoon."

I wasn't sure what the day would bring, but was fairly certain that our quest for the Ark would take multiple days. It was unlikely we would find anything on our first day of searching. The main goal I hoped to accomplish today was simply getting up on the slopes of the saddle so we could begin looking in the proper area. Even if we didn't find anything yet, I would feel like we've at least begun the expedition. Then, tomorrow we could start fresh from a position further up the mountain. The following days were likely to be tougher, though, since we'd be at a higher, colder elevation for an extended duration. How long I couldn't say; either until we found the Ark, until we ran out of food, or until the elements defeated us. I hoped, of course, that our expedition would have a successful end with the Ark located. It was entirely possible, however, that we would not find it and be forced to turn back. In fact, this was unfortunately the more probable outcome.

After finishing our coffee, we extinguished our cooking fire with dirt, making sure it was completely out. We rinsed off our cups and eating utensils, placing them back into our respective packs. Then, we proceeded to get dressed for the day, Martin and I putting on our now warm, dry clothing which had been heated by the fire earlier. Following this, we dismantled our tents, making sure to retrieve the stakes and tie-downs, packing them as neatly as possible into the tent bag which Martin then strapped to the outside of his pack. I had our camera and tripod mounted to my pack. We then double-checked that we had everything we needed safely stored. I made sure that some snacks and water were easily accessible so that I could get to them during our hike.

I also double-checked my CZ 75, hoping that I wouldn't actually need it, believing that it was simply just added insurance in case we ran into any problems. Given that we had survived the previous encounter with the Kurds, then we were probably good to go from this point onward. It was unlikely that anyone else would be on this side of the mountain at this time of year. In a strange way also, knowing that the Kurds were in the area actually provided an extra sense of security. Due to the Kurds, Turkish soldiers and ISIS militants were not likely to be lingering around; from the former we risked arrest and from the latter we faced certain death.

After getting our gear together and girding ourselves for the day, we gathered to pray. I found this shared ritual we had started beginning to be a source of reassurance. Not just because it was a way for me to take my concerns and thoughts to God, but - perhaps more meaningfully - it was a way for the four of us to commune in some small way as the Church. We may have differences with regards to our theology, our lives, our practices - yet, praying together we were truly united in Christ, with him in the midst of us. All the things which seemed so important to divide us in this life vanished, for a brief moment, during our prayer time together. I knew also that on the day of the resurrection, at Christ's return, we would receive in full what we experienced now in part.

We closed our common prayer with a request for God to protect us in our travels and made ready to head up the slopes.

CHAPTER NINETEEN

Upward

We hoisted our packs upon our backs and set off to begin our trek. I took one last glance behind me to get a glimpse of our now abandoned camp site. It had been a good evening there and provided much needed rest for this day's activity. I felt refreshed and eager to begin looking for the Ark. Knowing that we would be unlikely to find it on this first day of our expedition, I nevertheless was thankful to finally be able to actually begin the search for the object which the locals had reportedly seen, lying somewhere up ahead of us on the distant saddle.

The immediate ground in front of us was only slightly uphill. It was not a hard walk so far, but I could see further ahead that the going would soon get tougher as we progressed forward and the incline increased. We walked in single file with me leading, then Arman, followed by Martin and Yezras. We had all started to form a close bond together. As we walked, Arman and I shared stories from our home life and reflected, humorously, on the shared joys and tribulations of marriage and family across cultures. I could hear Martin and Yezras talking as well, they seemed to be sharing thoughts on hobbies, their plans for the future, and - of course - girls. It was both funny and encouraging that people everywhere have such similar hopes, dreams, and experiences.

We began to encounter steeper terrain as we went on, with small crags of ground popping up around us. There were a few places where we had to help each other around rocky obstacles. As we progressed we also found that we needed to cut an increasing number of switchbacks to make the ascent easier. This meant that our total distance traveled would be greater, but that our going would be less physically taxing. It seemed like a good tradeoff, since it was difficult to make too steep of a climb when encumbered with our packs and gear. Gravity's effects on our packs tended to want to pull us backwards when climbing.

We were still heading towards the saddle between the two mountain peaks, right between Greater Ararat and Lesser Ararat, the vicinity where the locals had reportedly seen the object after the earthquake. The present slopes on which we found ourselves would lead us up to our objective. We hoped we would make it there, much less find the reported object which we all hoped was actually the Ark. At the very least, we would be afforded a pleasant view of the peaks and the surrounding countryside. I hoped, though, for more than a picturesque tour. I wanted to see the Ark in person.

After a few hours of hiking up the increasingly difficult terrain, making as many switchbacks as necessary, we decided to stop to rest and eat lunch. We sat down on the rocky slope, not even bothering to take off our packs; we simply leaned back on them to use them as rests. Our lunch consisted of some crackers and dried beef jerky which we shared amongst us. We drank from our water supplies, having not yet arrived at the snow to replenish our stocks by melting some. I had also brought salt pills to help replace the electrolytes which had been lost through sweat during the hike so far. Even when it is cold outside, the body still perspires due to physical exertion. In fact, this tended to make a person feel worse, as once you stopped moving the dampness of your clothing made you feel even colder. Despite these drawbacks, though, we needed the rest and replenishment afforded to us by our lunch break.

We had gained some elevation in the few hours since we had set off, so the air was indeed beginning to get much colder. Last night the air had gotten chilly due to the setting of the sun, but now the air was cold even during the daylight hours. In a way, it was a welcome change from the warmer air we had experienced closer to the plain and in Nakhchivan. Now, the air was cool and crisp, with a slight breeze; as we exerted ourselves during our hike it was very welcome. It was still early in the day, however, and the sun was still to our southeast and therefore shining directly upon us. The hour would soon come when it would pass over to the other side of the mountains and then the two peaks would plunge us into their shadows. That, combined with the approaching even higher elevations, would serve to plunge the temperatures to below freezing.

"How much longer will we hike today?" Martin asked.

Arman answered, "We should try to get higher and then stop a few hours before nightfall to have time to make camp and build a fire. Tonight will be cold on the mountain."

"Maybe we can find a nice level spot in an outcropping as we go, and camp there," I said. It was more of a wish, I supposed. I was hoping we could find a location suitably sheltered from the winds and weather to rest during the long hours of darkness.

We finished our lunchtime break and resolved to continue with our ascent. We must have looked like overturned turtles as we attempted to get to our feet again to restart our hike. We paired together to help each other up through the leverage of our body weight; Martin and I grabbing hands to hoist each other up, Arman and Yezras doing the same. Once standing again we all let out a collective sigh and then started moving up the slopes. It was hard to get going.

I reminded myself not to think of anything but the present moment. Psychologically, thinking of either the end or the beginning of a journey only served to lessen one's resolve to continue. I had learned this from training for marathons. While running, if your thoughts wander to lying in bed back home or about being done with the race, then you simply just want to quit in order to go home and be done with it. But, if you could suppress these thoughts from your mind and just focus on the moment - putting one foot in front of the other - then, you would preserve the mental strength to keep going. Running a marathon was mostly a psychological test, really; once you had achieved a basic level of physical conditioning, then running 26.1 miles was a mental game. It was a similar situation here on this mountain. I knew I could physically make the hike and haul myself anywhere I wished to be on this mountain. To do so, though, I would have to keep focussed on the immediate moment and not allow my mind to wander back home or to the future.

When running, I always enjoyed listening to music or audio books in order to prevent my mind from thinking too much. I did not have such things to listen to on this hike, so I instead focused myself on the beauty of the terrain and landscape. I imagined the waters of the flood flowing down off the peaks of the mountain, carving the variations in the slopes on which we now trekked. I admired the little grasses and wildflowers which sprang up on our path. I peered into the distance to see the coming snow and its purity. My goal was to keep my mind occupied with thoughts which were unrelated to either being back home or being finished with this expedition. I tried my best to remain in the present, without wandering off to the past or into the future.

CHAPTER TWENTY

Snow and Fire

As we continued our ascent up the slopes, the ground underneath us grew steeper and rockier. We increasingly found ourselves having to struggle to get around or over obstacles at various points. Patches of snow finally began to appear as well, growing thicker and more abundant as we went along. Even though the temperature was dropping, I was happy to see the snow as it meant an endless supply of water, assuming we preserved the means to melt it.

When I was a kid, I had loved the snow. In all honesty, the main reason for my love was simply the opportunity to miss school. One time in elementary school I had nearly two weeks off school due to the continual snowfall which fell. Those were great times during which I had immense enjoyment from building forts, engaging in snowball fights, and simply spending hours outside with my friends. I suppose part of me still likes the snow, but I could see now that I would soon grow tired of it up here on this mountain, despite the ample supply of free, fresh water. We had just arrived within the outer perimeter of the snow fields, and soon we would be completely surrounded by the snow.

From past experience, the memory came back to me that snow gets in everything, working its way into boots, socks, waistbands, gloves, shirts, pants, hats - and then it melts. Once this happens, it makes continued existence out in the cold unpleasant, and creates difficulties with staying warm. As we entered into the deeper, more expansive snow fields, the snow would soon complete its awful mission by finding its way into my clothing, my pack, and - worst of all - my socks and boots. Then, it would melt and begin to re-freeze, making everything that much colder and the hike that much less enjoyable.

We had gained much greater elevation now which, combined with the sun passing over the peaks to the West, caused the temperature to drop, and it was starting to get very uncomfortable. The wind picked up and was brutal as well. Particles of rock and snow swept up by the gusts peppered my face as I trudged along up the slopes. I could feel my hands and ears getting colder. I finally fully buttoned up my coat and put on my hat and gloves, pulling the flaps of my hat down over my ears and propping up the collar on my coat to help protect my neck. Thankfully also, I had brought sunglasses with removable lenses, so I was able to take out the darker, tinted lenses and replace them with a clear set. I no longer needed protection from the sun, but from the wind and the particulates which it threw at me. As the wind beat against my face, I couldn't help but think of the greater coldness to come as darkness completely overtook us this evening.

"This is tough," said Yezras from the end of our little column.

I nodded in agreement. I couldn't see the others, but I imagined they all agreed as well. We were all experiencing this together. It wasn't even nightfall yet on the first day on the slopes, and we were already getting worn down by the weather.

It is such a strange feeling hiking in the mountains. As you ascend, the weather around you gets colder. However, your body gets hot from the exertion, and so you sweat. When you stop to rest, as eventually you must, the sweat either evaporates and makes you even colder, or it freezes - also making you colder. In a way, this is probably the worst part - having to stop - stopping just causes you to feel chilled to your very core once your cellular metabolism lessens and your body's heat output decreases. If only we could somehow just keep moving so we could stay warm. A fire would make stopping more endurable, at least. Thankfully, I suppose, we still had a few hours to go before we camped for the night.

We kept going in the only direction we really could - up. Although "up" also - unfortunately - meant that we also had to go sideways or laterally at times, continuing to cut switchbacks in order to soften the steepness of the ascent. The slopes continued to get steeper, and now the rocks were increasingly obscured by snow. This presented a new problem which I had not previously considered: knowing where to step. When I could see the rocks, I was able to avoid stepping directly on top of them, so that I didn't risk twisting my ankles by having a stone slip out from under my boot as I put my weight on it. With the snow cover, though, I couldn't see the rocks to avoid them. I hoped that there were no loose ones which would cause me, or the others in our party, to sprain something or fall.

As we went on it grew later in the day. I figured that we should start trying to find a good location to make camp for the evening, so I kept my eye out for a suitable location. Finally, I called out to the others, "Look there." I pointed them to a small plateau-like outcropping on the side of the mountain which I had spied, just up ahead and to the right of our path. The spot looked to be shielded from the wind and would be a good place to hole up for the night, I thought. The rear of the outcropping consisted of a nearly sheer wall which would block the wind, while the rest of it was flat and wide enough for our tents and a fire pit. A sharp cliff punctuated the end of the plateau.

Arman knew what I was thinking. "Yes," he answered, "that will make a fine spot for camp."

We headed over to our new home for the evening, reaching it by ascending upward and them moving laterally onto the plateau. The size and shape of the area afforded us the opportunity to position our tents in much the same way as at our previous campsite; parallel to each other with a fire pit in between. We dropped our packs and then pitched our tents, putting the heads of our tents closest to the sheer wall so that our feet would face towards the end of the plateau as we slept; the opening of the tents was therefore also facing the same direction. There was a space of nearly five feet from the end of the tents to the cliff, and the entire area was about twenty feet wide. This would be our home for the night, and we would pack up and abandon the site in the morning to continue our expedition.

After pitching our tents and placing our gear inside, we began collecting stones for the fire pit. This necessitated, of course, us searching underneath the snow for stones as well as clearing an area for the fire. A fire would be indispensable, both to warm us and for the psychological effect. The presence of fire when you are in the wilderness provides a level of consolation and peace which is out of proportion to the warmth and light which it provides. For the first time this realization really came home to me, as I began to light and then carefully tend our evening fire. It was quite a comfort as we sat by the flames, poking at the tinder and fuel we had brought along for the purpose in order to help the blaze grow in intensity and size.

I thought about the Lord's appearances in the Old Testament when He came to his people through fire;

first to Moses through the burning bush and later to the Israelites on Mount Sinai and in the desert through the pillar of fire. I pondered just what it meant that the Lord had appeared to His people through fire. It had been awe-inspiring to the people witnessing it; they feared the Lord and His power and might. However, the thought occurred to me now, as I sat by this fire on the mountain, that perhaps the Lord's fire was also meant as a comfort to His people. Through the fire, the Lord provided a visible and tangible demonstration that He was with them and would shelter and provide for them. They were not alone.

I knew I was not alone as well. The Lord was with us and would watch over us as we continued on our expedition. As I watched the embers emerge from the flames and ascend into the heavens, I imagined the awe with which the people of Israel beheld the fire from the Lord. Here I was, struggling in the cold, trying to make a fire, and being rewarded for my grand efforts with the first feeble hints of combustion, then the orange and blue flames as they grew in strength. God, however, can come down at will in fire anywhere He pleases: on a mountain, in a bush, on an altar (such as when Elijah called down fire in his contest with the priests of Baal). What a demonstrable presence and demonstration of power, I thought, to be able to make fire.

I felt a small sense of this power now on this mountain. We were thousands of miles away from home, consumed by the cold and soon to be engulfed by the coming darkness. But, I was able to make fire which would warm and comfort our small band. It would also be a symbol of the presence of the Lord among our group as we trusted in Him to guide and protect us. I continued to tend the fire. The tiny embers grew into larger ones and then finally into actual flames which began to consume the bits of tinder and wood which I had fed it.

Fire, like time, consumes all things. We build up grand designs and plans, and yet they are all eventually overtaken by time. I was in my mid-40s, having lived longer than I had imagined possible when I was but a child. It wasn't that I was exactly "old," but I did wonder how much longer I would have left in this present life. My son was less than half my age, with his whole life before him. Did he recognize this? Would he eventually be where I am, over 20 years from now, and wonder where the time went? Would he recognize how much the flames of time had consumed? Would he look back to his past, wishing he had done more, or look forward to the future, thankful for all that preceded?

Was that why I was here? I had told myself before that I had come to seek the Ark, to give some small measure of glory to God and to help convince others of His truth. Yet, now I wondered if this was really the primary reason. Had I, in fact, come here for myself? To convince myself that I was still "young" and had many years of life left in me; to not regret another missed opportunity?

We all ate dinner together as I pondered these questions in silence by the fire. I had no idea if the others had similar thoughts. Each of us seemed preoccupied by thought, or possibly just by the cold. After dinner we all prayed and then shuffled off to our tents and went to sleep, awaiting the sunrise and the dawn of the opportunity presented by a new day. Each day was a gift from God, and I was eager to see what the next morning's gift would be.

CHAPTER TWENTY-ONE

The Find

The first rays of sunlight illuminated our camp early in the morning as the radiance of the sun began to peek over the eastern plains below. We were on the east side of the mountain, high in elevation, allowing the beams easier access to us. As I awoke, I could see the light entering through the thin material of the tent. I shuffled out of my sleeping back and stumbled out of the tent, almost forgetting that the cliff was only a few feet away from the entrance. I was hit by the cold air of a slight breeze and confronted by a sky which looked like a painting of oranges, yellows, and reds. No one else was yet awake, so I stood on the precipice admiring the sunrise. First I saw just the rays of the sun. Then, slowly, the bright orb began to rise above the horizon. Initially it was just a sliver, but finally the entire beaming star was visible and shining across the plains to our east and up onto the leeward slopes of the mountain to us.

I reached back into the tent to get my boots, socks,

and hiking clothes. Despite my care and best efforts they had frozen over during the night due to the sweat of the previous day and the nightly frost. It was a disappointing development, but I figured I could dry and warm them by the fire as we ate breakfast. Martin woke up as I was inspecting my clothes, so I took the opportunity to warn him to be careful when he exited the tent, reminding him that the cliff was just a few feet away.

Arman and Yezras emerged from their tent as well. I saw them stretch and look around towards the horizon and then up towards the higher elevations of the slopes. They saw me and we wished each other a good morning as we set to work on getting our breakfast fire started. The flint and tinder we had brought with us succeeded after some effort in starting a fire, and Martin joined us by it.

I placed my clothes, boots, and socks near the fire, as did the others. We heated up some salted ham for breakfast and some water to mix with instant coffee grounds. A few crackers rounded out our meal. It took so little time to eat that our clothing had not yet dried out, so we continued to linger by the fire for a while longer, watching the sun rise ever higher above the horizon. Satisfied then that our clothing was as dry as it was going to get, we extinguished the fire and then changed into our now lukewarm hiking clothes. Following this we took down and packed our tents, collected all our gear, and then hoisted our packs upon our backs for another day of hiking. We really had no idea what the day would bring; we simply wanted to get moving.

We formed up into a small column and advanced off our little plateau to continue our ascent up the mountain. I was in front, Martin next, then Arman and Yezras. It was harder to get myself going this morning. It was cold, I was tired, and I had not slept very well during the night. I knew, though, that we had to keep going up if we had any hopes of finding the Ark. The longer we delayed, the more we sat on this mountain, the less chance we had of finding anything, or of making it off the mountain alive. In addition, the physical exertion would serve to warm my body as my metabolism kicked into gear. Indeed, after a few minutes of hiking I was again warm and felt more comfortable, even though I was tired. What helped me keep going was the thought of the unknown possibilities of the day.

On we went - up and laterally, continuing to cut switchbacks to assist ourselves with our ascent. The ground, like the latter part of our hike the day before, was covered in snow with rocks underneath. It was slow going and again necessitated careful navigation around or over obstacles as we encountered them. As of yet we had seen nothing of the Ark.

"Do you think we will find anything today, Mr. John?" asked Yezras.

"I don't know. It would be nice. We could then go home where it's warm and eat a celebratory meal," I joked.

The others let out weak laughs. The thought of going home was on all of our minds. We wanted to find the Ark first, though. I knew, however, that if we did manage to run across something which we thought was the Ark, it would mean spending a longer stretch on the mountain. For we would have to take some time to examine it to determine for certain what we had found. If it wasn't the Ark, then we'd have to keep looking. On the other hand, if it was the Ark we would need to explore it to the best of our ability. This itself would take some time. But, only God knew what we would find or if we would even find anything.

We hiked single-file for a couple of hours, moving carefully over rock and snow and continuing to have to cut switchbacks whenever the ground ahead was too steep. After awhile Arman thought he spotted something in the distance.

"Do you see that over there to the north?" he asked.

I pulled out my binoculars and looked to where he was pointing. There was a dark object, or shadow perhaps, running alongside the slope of the mountain, probably about 200 yards away to our right and at a slightly higher elevation. It could be a ship, but it was hard to tell from this distance.

"I see it," I answered. "Should we go take a

look?"

"It would be worth a look, I should think," said Arman.

We headed off in the direction of Arman's object. Unfortunately, there was no direct route to get there due to the terrain; between us and it were numerous caverns and crevices. Therefore, we had to climb some more, then traverse the slopes laterally as much as we could, then alternatively ascend and descend around many obstacles, trying our best to make as much progress as possible towards the object. It took us quite a while, but we finally made it over to what Arman had seen.

Upon first inspection, it looked like a large rock formation pressed into the side of the earth, approximating the shape of a large boat. It was hundreds of feet long, lying lengthwise parallel to the slopes, with its width of a few dozen yards running laterally. The edges, or rim, rose about three or four feet above the rest of the surface of the mountainside.

We all wondered aloud whether this could be the Ark. We moved around the near-side perimeter of the object the best we could, climbing over rocks and digging snow away with our pickaxes in order to get a closer look at what lie underneath. We then crossed over to the far side of the object, taking pains to look carefully at the ground as we went to try to determine just what it was we were exploring. At various points we cleared the snow to again see what it was hiding. So far the only thing we had discovered under the snow was rock. This was further confirmed upon getting to the other side and examining the "rim" of the structure, it looked to be simply more rock.

"I don't think this is it," I finally said. I had hoped this would be the Ark, but realized that it was a false hope. There was no ship in this spot.

"Why not?" asked Martin.

"It looks to just be a rock formation, like many others on these mountains. Like the one we explored the other day at our base camp."

"I agree," sighed Arman. "There is no evidence of wood or anything man-made. It is just rock."

It was disappointing, but on the bright side we had at least found something worth exploring. That made me happy in some respects. Unfortunately, in so doing we had worn ourselves out and expended much of the day. I was tired, and I knew the others were as well. In addition, the sun had already crossed over to the other side of the mountains and dusk would soon arrive. Therefore, I suggested that we stay here for the evening.

"Should we camp here in this spot for the night? It's getting late and this offers some shelter from the wind, due to the rock walls of the formation."

They all agreed, so we found the most level spot possible and made camp in the same layout as we had previously. This time, though, we didn't have to worry about a cliff at the foot of our tents. We also had much more room for our camp. We pitched our tents parallel to each other, a few feet apart, and again made a fire pit between them. For the fire pit, we cleared an area of snow and placed a circle of rocks, placing our metal rack above the pit for cooking, as was our usual pattern. The tent stakes were difficult to drive into the ground, but we did the best we could. They were shallowly placed, but the weight of our packs inside would keep the tents in place and steady.

After making camp we took some time to rest within our tents. Martin took a short nap, while I read more of the Bible I had brought with me. This time I read St. Peter's First Epistle. His words in chapter 3, in particular, stood out to me in light of our expedition:

For Christ also suffered once for sins, the righteous for the unrighteous, that he might bring us to God, being put to death in the flesh but made alive in the spirit, in which he went and proclaimed to the spirits in prison, because they formerly did not obey, when God's patience waited in the days of Noah, while the ark was being prepared, in which a few, that is, eight persons, were brought safely through water.

Baptism, which corresponds to this, now saves you, not as a removal of dirt from the body but as an appeal to God for a good conscience, through the resurrection of Jesus Christ, who has gone into heaven and is at the right hand of God, with angels, authorities, and powers having been subjected to him.

Peter compares the salvation of Noah across the waters in the Ark to baptism. Baptism saves us on account of Christ's death and resurrection. Christ died for our sins and then rose to life; he raises us to new life in him through baptism where we receive his salvation. Thus, we are brought through the waters to a new life, much as Noah was. The instrument of salvation in Noah's case was the Ark. In our case the "ark" is the Church; she is the one who rebirths us into new lives with Christ through God's Word with the waters of Baptism. Peter makes the connection that Noah's Ark and the flood was a symbol or sign of what was to come with Christ.

After finishing Peter's epistle (it's not long) it was time for dinner. I woke Martin from his nap, and we exited our tent. Arman and Yezras were already outside; they had further explored the immediate area around our camp while we had been resting.

"Did you see anything?" I asked them.

"Not anything of interest," answered Arman. "We did find a good track out of this formation which we can follow tomorrow. It is just a short way up the slopes and will take us out of the rim so we can continue our climb."

"Thank you. That will be good. Should we make

dinner for tonight?"

Everyone heartily agreed, the day's exertions having given rise to hunger in all of us. We started a fire, gently nursing the first embers into ever larger flames until we had something substantial which generated much light and warmth. We heated up some preserved beef, eating that along with portions of Arman's bread. Thankfully, we now also had plenty of available fresh water, due to the snow. I had brought some lime juice which we mixed with our water so as to get some vitamin C into our systems as well as to give the water a hint of flavor. I had always thought that lime is refreshing, tasting clean and crisp.

After eating, we continued to recline by the fire. As we did so, we discussed the day's events and what lay before us tomorrow and possibly the next few days. We anticipated much hiking on terrain which was steeper and more difficult to traverse than that which we had previously encountered. As a result, spirits were not as high as they had been earlier in the day; the fatigue and cold were beginning to get to us, wearing us down both mentally and physically. Tomorrow would likely wear us down even more.

Our moments together by the fire helped, though, in some small way to encourage us. This interval of fellowship and communion served to reconfirm our shared commitment to our expedition and our determination to see it through. Even with the hardships, we could not see ourselves turning back yet. There was still much more of the mountain to explore, and we had only just begun to reach the saddle between the peaks. Since we faced a big day of hiking in the morning, we all resolved to get as much rest as we could that night so that we could start fresh in the morning.

After our time of dinner and discussion was over we followed our now routine pattern of extinguishing the fire, praying together, and then heading off into our tents for sleep. Martin and I entered our tent and bid each other goodnight. I, however, lay awake for quite some time, thinking about what tomorrow might bring. Would we finally find the Ark? Would it just be another day of fruitless searching? As I had observed the previous night, each day was a gift, so I would have to wait until the morning to see what God would give.

CHAPTER TWENTY-TWO

Searching

We were again woken early by the rising sun. This morning, however, we were given a slight reprieve due to the rim of the rocky ship-like formation in which we had slept; the rim blocked part of the horizon, causing the sun's rays to take a little longer to reach us. As dawn broke, light shone through the tent, urging Martin and I to arise for the day. This we did, I exiting the tent first while Martin attempted to shake off the previous evening's sleep. He would follow in a few moments.

Emerging from the tent, I stretched and looked outward to the horizon. The sunrise was amazing, even better than the previous morning. Today there were swaths of pink, orange, and purple across the eastern sky. I had seen beautiful sunrises many times in my life, but this one was something special. It seemed to have texture to it, like the merging of a painting with the object which the painting was meant to depict. The light glimmered off the snow fields, giving them a translucent quality.

Martin soon joined me in admiring the scene. "It's quite a sunrise," he said. "How many more do you think we'll see up here?"

"I'm not sure. We'll try to ascend the mountain some more today and maybe move a bit more sideways along the slopes to see if we can find anything worth checking out. We'll at least be able to cover additional ground today and eliminate some areas from our search. I've been marking off the areas we've traveled on our maps."

As Martin and I were talking, Arman and Yezras emerged from their tent and came and stood by us. They also commented on the sunrise and asked what our plan was for today. I suggested what I had previously told Martin, and they agreed. In truth, there really wasn't any other realistic plan; we either had to keep moving around on the mountain, trying to locate the Ark, or turn back. Determined to keep going, we therefore made our morning fire in the fire pit. This morning we heated up salted ham, eating that along with some crackers and our obligatory instant coffee. I warmed my clothes by the fire again as we ate. After breakfast we cleaned up our campsite, packed our tents and gear, and broke camp.

We first set off for the higher portion of the formation in which we had camped. After twenty or thirty minutes we reached its rocky rim and scrambled over it to exit the depression in which we had camped. Now we were on the main part of the slope and continued our ascent the best we could. Our climb, as it had been on the previous day, was punctuated by switchbacks to make the going easier, but longer. The circuitous route combined with the increasing amounts of snow served to slow our progress.

It was a cold, windy morning. The snow, picked up by the wind, struck my face like a harsh sandblast. Thankfully, though, by now my beard was starting to come in with some fullness, which helped to protect and warm my face. All of us, even the boys, had beards - to a greater or lesser degree. Mine and Arman's were tinged with gray, while the boys' were dark black. As we hiked, I found it relaxing to stroke my beard periodically through my gloved hand. For some reason, the beard also made me feel wiser and stronger. I thought it was interesting how such a small physical change could have such an extensive psychological impact; little hairs growing on my face altered my outlook. It was amazing that our minds are so affected by our bodies.

Maybe this should not be so surprising, though? We are, after all, physical creatures. We are not just souls, but bodies as well. This is how God made us as humans: both body and soul united in one person. Perhaps this is why so many things of God are associated with physical elements which we can touch or see or taste? I thought of the Church's Baptism in which God's Word comes with the water; the Lord's Supper in which the Lord comes with the bread and wine; the Lord himself, actually, who came in the flesh to save us. The Lord approaches us in ways in which we - as embodied creatures - can receive Him. The Church herself is nothing if not flesh and blood people, and is actually called "the body of Christ." In the Apostles' Creed, too, the Church confesses that she believes in the resurrection of the body and the life everlasting. We don't believe in an eternity as disembodied souls, but rather as restored people, both body and soul. God created us as humans and will resurrect our bodies, reuniting them with our souls, so that we can dwell with Him forever as the humans He created us to be. Thus, it made sense in light of these truths that our mental state is affected by the condition or state of our bodies.

I suppose this is also why our spirits are affected by our physical surroundings. Beautiful sunrises make us feel happy and hopeful. Rainy days make us feel tired and, often, depressed. Bright colors make us anxious, while cool colors make us relaxed. Our bodies are an intimate part of who we are. We cannot divorce ourselves from them. God created us as both body and soul, and - try as we might - we cannot separate the two. In fact, God does not intend for them to remain separated even at death; that is why He promises the resurrection.

As we continued to hike through this mountain range I reflected on how, back home, I had always found running so relaxing and fulfilling. To be able to run a half-marathon or full marathon filled me with a sense of accomplishment and helped me to emotionally feel better. Now on this mountain, with each exertion of my body I felt my soul refreshed. In a strange way I felt that I was more human here. I had the opportunity to work my body to the point of exhaustion, which only served to drive my mind to ever deeper levels of thought.

We scrambled across the slopes of the mountain, moving progressively upwards and laterally, looking for another spot worthy of further investigation. Around mid-morning, we stopped for a short lunch of jerky, resting on our packs on the side of the mountain. Then, after our brief break we pressed on. Every now and then one of our party would spot something in the distance which we thought looked interesting, so we would all work our way towards the point of interest, only to be disappointed by yet another rock formation, or crevice, or drift of snow which - from afar - had looked like it might be our goal. Each false find caused us to feel even more discouraged with our odds of ever finding the Ark. The positive outlook which I had developed earlier in the day began to wane with each unsuccessful find and as the hour grew late.

As the day drew on, I came to the disheartening realization that we were going to have to spend another night on the mountain. My spirits dropped at the thought. I was already cold and tired, and I knew the rest of our group was as well. We all hoped to find the Ark, but wanted to find it on our own timeline, and that timeline could be classed as "immediately." God wasn't cooperating, though, and it was starting to occur to me with greater clarity that perhaps we would not find anything at all. I knew this was a possibility all along, of course, but my sense of optimism had managed to suppress it. Now, with fatigue taking over my body the sense of hope which I had maintained so far was starting to fail me. Indeed, it came to mind that one of the many boat-shaped rock formations we had explored previously on this mountain could very well have been the object which the locals had reportedly seen after the earthquake. These formations looked ship-like from a distance; we may have actually already found the locals' object without knowing it. We may have been led up here, in the cold and snow, chasing after rocks.

Since it was getting late in the day, though, I had to discard these thoughts and focus on our most immediate need; we had to find a decent place to make camp as the day would soon give way to night and the temperature would drop drastically.

Arman apparently had come to the same conclusion: "The weather will get worse soon. We must find a place to stay for the night and we shall begin again in the morning."

We started looking around for a spot which would afford us some relative screening from the elements. Unfortunately, in the area in which we presently were there were no level spots of ground or protective outcroppings. Therefore, we continued to hike for a while with the sole purpose of locating a suitable spot for camp. The wind picked up, driving waves of snow dust in our faces as we sought shelter. It was also getting worryingly late in the day. These factors urged us to seek any place which was even remotely adequate; we had no time to find a perfect spot. Thus, after some additional searching we identified an acceptable spot for camp. It was a small outcropping, about ten feet square on each side. It did not protect us much from the wind, nor was it very level, but it would have to do.

We attempted to pitch our tents, but the ground was just too rocky to drive the stakes through; and, unlike the previous evening, the wind was too high to leave the tents untethered. Thus, after many frustrating attempts at setting up the tents, we decided to give up. We would spend the evening in our sleeping bags out on the elements, collecting ourselves together into the closest formation we could so that our bodies would act as a common shield against the wind and falling temperatures. It would be a cold night, offering only fitful rest.

A fire was out of the question as well. It was much too windy to attempt to build one. We therefore contented ourselves with more jerky and some crackers as we all bundled ourselves in our sleeping bags. I had never thought I'd get tired of eating jerky, but I had now reached that point. My teeth and jaws were worn out from trying to chew it, and my lips were so dry and cracked that my own blood intermingled with anything I ate or drank.

I retrieved some canned fuel from my pack to help us melt snow to replenish our water supplies. We all huddled around the ridiculously small flame which the humble can provided. But, it was something at least. The tiny flames served to warm our spirits at least a little. Long after we had melted enough snow for our needs we still sat by that humble fire, huddled in our bags, until the fuel finally ran out and the fire extinguished itself. We then said a short prayer together, asking for the Lord's protection during the night, and then lay down in our sleeping bags, not even bothering to remove our hiking clothes or change into something else. It was much too cold to do so. As we lay on the mountain side, we were a mass of shivering men.

I buried myself into my sleeping bag as far as I could and pulled the drawstring tight around my head. The others did the same; we must have all looked like mummies buried in the snow. I could imagine us dying on the mountain and being found thousands of years from now as people debated our identities and our manner of death, and put forward all sorts of absurd theories about our lives and reasons for being here on these slopes. I prayed that we would be alright during the night. It was so incredibly cold that I did my best to cover as much of my body by the bag as I could. Only my eyes peeked out of the slot provided by the bag; my breathing was labored since the rest of my head was buried within.

As night fell I could see an innumerable number of stars through my little viewing slot. Back home it was hard to see many stars at night due to the light from the city which polluted the sky. Here, though, there were no competing lights, so the beauty of the nocturnal signs above could shine through the firmament to be perceived by my eyes. The moon - the "lesser light" created by God - and the constellations of Aries, Taurus, and Triangulum loomed overhead in the midst of a sea of celestial bodies. I remembered God's promise in the Old Testament to Abraham to make his descendants as many as the "stars of heaven" and the New Testament's elucidation that all those who have faith in Christ are actually Abraham's descendants. As I surveyed this sign in the heavens I thought of the four of us on this mountain. We were among those whom God promised Abraham; children of faith who - tonight more than ever - needed our Lord's protection as we trembled on the mountain of Noah. I prayed that the Lord would send the morning quickly so that we could again be warmed, even if ever so slightly, by the rays of the "greater light" which He had placed in the heavens.

CHAPTER TWENTY-THREE

The Fall

Due to the uncomfortableness of the freezing air, I awoke well before dawn. In fact, I hadn't slept well at all during the night. The weather and the hard ground made it too intolerable to get much rest. Upon waking, I tried to bury myself even deeper into my sleeping bag to stay warm. However, after a while I made two realizations: I was not going to be able to go back to sleep and I was not going to get any warmer in the bag. So, I decided to go ahead and get up and start moving around our campsite to try to generate some body heat which might serve to raise my temperature.

Thus, I crawled out of my bag into the night sky. The stars were still clear above, and the wind was still whipping against my face. I rolled up my sleeping bag to try to prevent snow from entering, then began to pace around our little campsite. I must have looked ridiculous, walking as I was in a tight circle in an attempt to warm myself. It started to work, though. Soon I was not nearly as cold as I had been.   Rather than being completely frozen, I now felt like "warmed over" leftovers.

The environment and the fitful night of sleep had taken its toll on me. Between thoughts of how cold it was and how uncomfortable I was, I kept wondering if we should just head back down the mountain today. We had searched in vain for the Ark so far and were not likely to find it. Maybe it'd be better if we simply returned while we still had the strength to do so?   It would be much easier to descend down the mountain, and we could avoid as many switchbacks as possible to make it to the base of the mountain before nightfall.

I thought of my home and my wife and daughter. I missed them deeply and wished to see them. Thoughts of warm weather, cold beer, and steak and potatoes also entered my mind. How I missed those as well!   The cold, snow, jerky, salted ham, and crackers of our expedition were growing old and I was sick of them. I now longed to return home and get off this blighted mountain.

A few days ago, I had resolved to remain "in the moment" and not allow thoughts of the beginning or end of the expedition to invade my mind, knowing that they would inevitably cause me to want to turn back. I realized that I had now failed in this regard.   Each thought of home simply served to make me covet the end of this journey; the quickest way of being done, of course, was to walk down off this mountain today. On the one hand, I still wanted to find the Ark, but on the other hand, the siren's call of home lured me even stronger. My will to continue the expedition was faltering.

After what seemed like an eternity of pacing in circles, but which was probably only an hour or so, I spotted the first strands of light shooting up from the horizon. As I stared, more and more light came into view until, finally, the outermost rim of the sun's orb peeked above the plains below. Thank God it was finally morning. Now, at least, some comparative warmth would come and perhaps the light would brighten my spirits.

The others awoke as the rays touched them, and they crawled out of their sleeping bags. The cold air seemed to shock them as they left the relative protection of their bags. Everyone shivered with crossed arms, trying their best to stay warm as they paced about.

I pulled Martin aside.

"Do you think we should head back?" I asked him.

"No, I want to keep going. We've come so far. We can't give up now."

"I don't know, Martin. We've been looking for days and have nothing to show for it. We can't stay up here forever, eventually we do need to return home. At what point do we decide that there's nothing here for us to find?"

"I know," he said. "But, it's too soon to turn back."

"Son, I don't know how many more nights like last night I can endure up here."

Martin thought for a moment. "Dad, we've come so far to be here and have already gone further than we thought we could. We can't go back now. Let's give it some more time. We're not even to the top of the saddle yet."

I stood silent, thinking. It was true that we were further than we thought we'd be. There would also never be another opportunity to come here and look for the Ark. As much as I hated to acknowledge it, Martin was probably right. I was thankful - in this case - for youth's impetuousness which served to urge us onward.

"Ok, but I should talk with Arman as well."

Arman was rolling up his sleeping back, while Yezras - next to him - did the same.

"Arman," I said as I tapped him on his shoulder. He stood to face me. I continued, "You don't have to do this. If you and Yezras wish to turn back, I understand. I'd like to go back myself, but Martin and I will keep looking for the Ark. This need not be your quest."

* * *

He seemed visibly insulted, standing even more upright as he responded to me. "Never will I or my son turn back as long as you and your son are on this mountain. We will keep going with you. It has become our quest as well. Now, let us eat quickly and break camp so we can make the most of the day."

We ate a cold breakfast of jerky, skipping the coffee for today in our haste to get moving, both to warm ourselves as well as to begin our search. As we ate we put our sleeping bags in our packs and prepared to move out. The uncomfortable night had put a finer point on the need to search as much as the slopes as possible before we were forced by the weather, our dwindling supplies, and our falling spirits to give up and go back down this mountain. Thus, after packing our gear and hoisting our packs upon our backs we headed off again, using much the same strategy as we had employed the previous day; moving both up and laterally at various points so as to get a good view of the slopes and cover as much ground as we possibly could.

After hiking for a few minutes we set as our immediate target a rock formation which we had spotted in the distance. It was above us on the slopes and to our right side - towards Greater Ararat - a few hundred yards. The formation looked interesting mainly because it blocked our view of what was beyond it. We figured that if we could reach it then we would be afforded a better view of the rest of the slopes which lie on the other side. Due to the difficulty of the intervening terrain, it would take us a couple hours to make it there, so we moved as quickly as we could.

Stumbling over the snowy, rocky terrain we made slow progress towards the formation. Fatigue forced us to stop a few times to regain our strength. However, we kept pressing onward, happy at least to have a goal in sight. There may be nothing to see on the other side of the formation, but I wasn't worried about that possibility at the moment. I focused my thoughts on simply reaching our destination; I had no plan for what came after that. I was too tired to think of anything else, other than keeping on the move. At this elevation - nearly fourteen thousand feet - I could barely get enough of the thin air into my lungs as I needed and was constantly out of breath.

After a long, difficult hike we had nearly reached the formation. As we closed the distance to it, we could see that it was a craggy spur coming down from the main ridge line. It was a good thirty feet high, so we searched for an accessible spot in which to attempt to ascend to the top of it. After moving parallel to the side of the spur for a number of yards, we eventually found a point where its cliff wall was not quite so vertical. However, it was still too steep to even make our way up it using switchbacks. Thankfully, we had brought climbing gear with us, so Martin and I retrieved our ropes and equipment from our packs. We all fastened makeshift harnesses to ourselves and then began the climb.

Martin was the better climber, so he went first, followed by Arman and Yezras; I brought up the rear. We had carabiners attached to our harnesses with a rope connecting us all together. Martin make sure to affix anchors as he advanced upwards to help protect us from a potential fall. We all struggled to the top. Even though it was not too terribly far, the topography and the bulkiness of our gear made it difficult. After nearly half an hour of struggling, Martin managed to reach the top and then was able to assist us in reaching the height of the spur as well.

The wind was much stronger up here, since we had lost what little shielding we had enjoyed previously due to the cover provided by the side of the mountain. Standing on this spur which protruded out from the main slope, we were now able to see what lie beyond. On the other side of the spur, opposite the direction from which we had come, was a large fissure in the earth. It was a few hundred yards distant and ran perpendicular to the saddle between the two peaks of Ararat. It appeared that it might have been caused by the earthquake; it seemed "fresh." It was also situated such that a person standing at the right location down on the plains below would likely be able to see it. It seemed like as good a place as any to explore up here. Accordingly, we decided to head towards it to check it out.

We descended down the other side of the spur

from which we had come in order to get down to the main slope nearest the fissure. We then made our way laterally across the slopes towards it. After a long, arduous trek we finally reached it. It was then that we noticed that this fissure began as a crack in the earth and soon grew into a wide gulf as it went further up the mountain and into the saddle. We chose to explore the area, taking the nearer side of the expanse as our guide, intending to move upwards towards the wider sections above. We therefore entered into the expanse, descending down a wall of earth and rock a few yards deep and finding a narrow path on which we could hike; the other side of the path dropped off into the deeper sections of the fissure.

Beginning our exploration, we were soon scrambling over boulders and staggering over crevices which the earthquake had apparently opened in the earth. These obstacles made it slow going. As we continued our ascent along its side, the gulf in the earth grew wider and deeper still. It was now hundreds of yards wide and dozens of yards deep. Unlike the rest of the slopes, there was less snow within the gulf, so we could see the rock and earth within.

"Do you think this is what the locals saw?" Martin asked.

"Maybe," I answered. "It's certainly large enough and in the right position to be seen from down below. I wonder, though, if they actually saw the Ark in here, or if they just saw the shadows of this fissure from a distance and reported that. I'm sure that the relatively snowless feature of this place, compared with the snow of the surrounding areas, makes it stand out from a distance."

"Hopefully it's not just the shadows they saw and that they really did see something."

Arman had a suggestion, "We should try to get to the top of this break in the earth and then make our way around the top to the other side to search from there."

The top seemed to be nearly a mile ahead of us; this was a huge distance considering the difficulty of the terrain. This would be a long day indeed. To get around this gulf, cross over it, and then start searching around the other side would take a lot of effort. However, this was probably what was necessary. This expanse in the earth was too wide to effectively see everything from just one side. Compounding the problem was the fact that there were also numerous secondary formations within it which prevented a clear view into its recesses.

So we went on, with me in the lead and our small column behind. Soon the earth began to hem us in. To our left was the wall of the formation and the escalating cliffs of the mountains. To our right was the expanding gulf of earth opened up by the earthquake. We had only two ways to go, up or down. Therefore, we kept going up towards our destination. What else could we do? Earlier this morning I had wanted to quit and go back, but now that we had found something interesting and worth exploring I wanted to go on. To go down would be to give up on this quest and admit defeat. Defeat by what, though? This mountain? Circumstances? How often in our lives, I thought, do we let circumstances defeat us when, if only we kept going, there would be an end in sight for all those difficulties which had disheartened us. I determined that this would not be one of those times in which I let circumstances turn me back from a greater hope. Despite my earlier desire this morning to go home, I pressed forward now, certain that we would soon find something else worth finding which was worthy of the effort.

The hemming in of the ground around us became more severe. We had less flat space in which to walk as the ascending and descending cliff walls on either side of us edged ever closer together. What had started as a path of about six feet wide now narrowed to no more than a foot wide. Our packs scraped the cliff wall to our left, and occasionally our right feet found themselves perched partway over the cliff to our right. Nevertheless, we shuffled along upward, heading towards the top of the formation. Pebbles and loose earth on the ground made it even harder to keep a footing.

Suddenly, I heard someone scream from behind me. Stopping and turning to look back, I saw Arman and Yezras gaping over the cliff edge which emptied into the gulf. My heart sank - I didn't see Martin! I looked down below to where the others were pointing.

Down about ten yards below us lay Martin. He had apparently slipped off the edge of our path and fallen down into the gulf. Thankfully, the ground underneath at this point was not a sheer drop, and he had landed on a small ledge on the side of the cliff. This ledge was situated above a deeper section of the gulf which, by this time, had grown into its own valley of sorts.

Martin was on his side and didn't seem to be moving. I could see blood running out from underneath his head.

We needed to find a way to get down to him quickly.

CHAPTER TWENTY-FOUR

The Descent

"We're coming!" I yelled down to Martin, not knowing if he was conscious and could hear me. He was still motionless. I hoped and prayed that he was alive and ambulatory. I had no idea what we'd do if he had broken something, especially a foot or a leg. How would we get him off this mountain? It had taken all our strength, and limbs, to get to where we now were. It would be extremely difficult to stretcher someone off of this mountain. It would also significantly extend the time required for our descent.

Arman offered assistance as he shuffled closer to me, "Here, get the rope from my pack." There wasn't much room to maneuver, but he was able to turn his back towards me so that I could access his backpack to retrieve the rope which he had brought. Coiling the rope in my hands, it occurred to me that it was all well and good to have a rope, but there were no trees on which to tie it to lower ourselves down to Martin, nor was the ground conducive to setting anchors.   We would have to make do, however. There was no other option.

I looked at Arman, "Do you think you and Yezras could use your bodies to anchor the rope as I go down it to Martin?"

"Yes," they both answered in unison without hesitation.

Crammed in as we were between the cliff wall and the ledge, Arman and Yezras had to do their best to prepare themselves to hold my body weight on the other end of the rope.   They braced themselves side-by-side as they wrapped the rope around themselves. Yezras was in front, so to speak, nearest me. His physically larger father Arman was behind him; together they would be my repelling anchor. Yezras tied the end of the rope in a slip knot in front of him. My weight on the other end of the rope would tighten the knot around the both of them.   Hopefully, they could hold all of over 200 pounds of me without falling themselves, or getting burned or lacerated by the rope. I figured that their coats would afford them some protection from the rope's effects.   Regardless, they would only have to support me for a short time.

I hadn't really thought about the end game yet, though.   Once I got down to Martin, how would I get him and myself back up to Arman and Yezras? Not knowing or caring for the moment what the solution to this problem was, I threw the other end of the rope over the edge and down the cliff into the gulf.   Its end coiled next to Martin on the ledge below.   Then, I grabbed the rope with both hands and gently lowered myself over the edge as Yezras and Arman strained to support my weight.   Once I was over, I wrapped my right foot around the rope to use it as a break to help slow my descent.   As I proceeded down to Martin, my two anchors did their best to maintain their position on the rocky ground, leaning backward against the wall of the cliff and wedging their feet against the larger rocks nearest the edge in front of them. Struggling, they used all their weight and strength to keep from being pulled off the side by me as I descended down the rope.

Hurrying along the rope as fast as I safely could, in a few seconds I had completed the descent to the ledge on which Martin had fallen. I knelt beside him to check his condition, hoping that he was alright. He was breathing, and the only obvious injury I saw was a gash to his head. Blood was flowing freely, but thankfully I already saw the first signs of clotting.

"Martin! Martin!" I gently shook him.

To my great relief, he began to rouse. He rolled over onto his back and looked at me. "Nice of you to drop by," he said, letting out a weak chuckle.

I laughed, and he smiled.   It was good to have Martin back.

"Are you hurt? It looks like you hit your head."

* * *

He reached up and felt the wound on his head and observed the resulting blood on his hand. Although bleeding profusely, the wound appeared superficial; it could be patched up easily enough with some bandages.

"I feel ok. Let me try to get up."

"Wait, let me check your legs and feet first," I said.

I looked carefully at his legs and rotated his feet to make sure there were no breaks or sprains. Being satisfied that - other than his head - he was alright, I helped Martin to his feet. Miraculously, he had not broken anything in the fall. I looked up to the edge from where he had fallen and noticed that a few feet below it the ground actually sloped downwards to this ledge, rather than being a sharp drop. He must have rolled down this incline, saving himself from breaking any bones or suffering a worse injury. It was also very fortunate that his fall managed to stop at this ledge, for on the other side was a cliff with a more extensive drop.

I yelled up to Yezras and Arman that Martin was ok, and saw them smile and wave in response. They still held the rope, so I thought that we could use it to climb back to them, even though it meant that they would again have to serve as anchors. I was preparing to help Martin make his ascent when I decided to go back to the edge of where we now stood to take another look into the gulf which opened up underneath this ledge. As I peered below, I observed that this ledge had shielded the view into the gulf from above, so from this new vantage point I could get a better look into the secrets which were held by the earth.

That's when I saw it.

CHAPTER TWENTY-FIVE

Spotted

As I peered over and beneath the side of the ledge something caught my eye. I stared, unable to turn away. Martin came over to where I was in order to see what I was looking at. He began to stare as well, caught up in the same mesmerizing sight. At first, though, I wasn't sure exactly what I saw. It almost looked like a huge - I mean gigantic - rib cage. Then, I realized that it was the hull of a wooden ship. Portions of the upper decking and side planking were missing, allowing a view into the ship and its structural ribs, giving it the appearance of a great wooden rib cage.

The closest point of the ship was about twenty yards below, and it seemed to be situated parallel with the sides of the fissure or gulf in the earth. That is to say that it was lying perpendicular to the top of the mountain, cuddled within the gulf, resting at a slight angle. I couldn't tell which end was the bow and which was the stern, as the ends were still covered by earth, as was the very bottom of the ship around the sides. The hull was slightly curved, but overall of a rectangular shape. Its color was a very dark, mottled brown. The wood had an aged and well-worn appearance, like reclaimed wood from an old barn.

My eyes traced the ship's length. It ran hundreds of feet up and down the gulf which had been opened by the earthquake. I could only surmise that the tremor had shaken off the snow and earth which had covered the ship, finally revealing the secret which had remained concealed here for thousands of years. This was the Ark. I could hardly believe it! It was actually here, still preserved in the spot where legend had placed it and circumstances had revealed it.

I was finally able to look away from the sight and turn to Martin. His face also contained the look of absolute amazement, which slowly turned into a wide smile. "Is that what I think it is? Am I awake or dreaming?"

"You're most definitely awake, and that is what you think it is. Let's get Arman and Yezras down here with us so we can all make our way down to the Ark and check it out in person. They're not going to believe this."

We yelled up to them to come to us. They seemed confused, since the view from where they were afforded no glimpse of the Ark. I imagine they must have thought it important, though, so they proceeded to descend to where Martin and I were. Arman held the rope while Yezras descended to our little ledge. Yezras informed his father of the gentle hidden slope underneath him; this was the same which had broken Martin's fall earlier. Thus, Arman coiled up the rope, took a leap of faith onto the slope which he could not see, and then carefully climbed down the bank to us.

Once they reached the ledge with us, we pointed to the Ark below, not yet telling them what we had found. However, from this new observation point they immediately realized what we had called them down for. I watched their faces as they spotted the Ark. They had the same mixture of shock and disbelief written upon them, soon changing into smiles as well.

"Dearest Savior," exclaimed Arman. "The Ark really is here!" We were all extremely joyful, hugging and slapping each other on the back in celebration. After such a hard trek up the slopes of this mountain and through all the doubt and difficulties, we had actually found the Ark. We were elated, and this elation overcame our fatigue. It was getting late in the day, but we were ready to immediately explore our new find. There was not a moment to lose.

Of course, actually getting down from our present position to the Ark would be difficult. It was lying below us at a distance too far to jump and too difficult to climb down directly. We would have to repel down to it. Once again our rope would come in handy, if we could find a suitable anchor. There was no way we could leave Arman up here to hold the rope, since it appeared impossible for him to later make his way down to us by himself.

"We need to find something to tie or lodge the rope to, so we can get down to the Ark and back up safely, if we can't find another way off the Ark and out of the gulf later," I said.

We all looked around our ledge. In truth, there wasn't much to look for; the area wasn't that big. We did find, though, a large boulder next to the slope, underneath the higher shelf from which we had descended earlier. The boulder allowed a sliver of access to its far side; there appeared to be enough room to pass the rope through it. Thus, we could tie the rope around it, using it as an anchor; once done, the rope would not be able to slip off the boulder, as it was wedged directly underneath the wall of the cliff above it. Satisfied therefore that this would make an excellent anchor point, we wrapped the rope around the boulder, tying it in front. It would be our lifeline down to the Ark and, most likely, back up again once we were ready to make our way down the mountain.

I turned to the others, "I'll stay here and monitor the rope while you go down to the Ark, and then I'll come down after you." Even though the rope was suitably secured, I figured it would be wise to guard it during the others' descent, just in case the knot came loose or the anchor somehow proved unsure. I considered too that since Arman and Yezras had anchored the rope previously when I came down to this ledge, the least I could do now was perform a similar function for them. This would also serve to allow the others the honor of preceding me to the Ark.

Thus, Arman, Yezras, and Martin prepared for their descent while I stood by the boulder. As Arman made his descent first, I carefully watched the rope; everything seemed to be fine. After Arman reached the Ark, he made sure that the landing spot was secure and stable. Satisfied that it was, he yelled up the all-clear. Yezras was the next to descend, followed by Martin. Finally, I went down as well.

What I saw when I got down to the others was absolutely incredible.

CHAPTER TWENTY-SIX

Exploration

Our landing spot from the repel down the ledge was on what must have been the roof of the Ark. There was a ragged hole in the roof in front of us, through which I could see vast beams of wood and decking inside the ship below us. There were many such openings in the roof which I could see, and the entire Ark was no longer in one undisturbed piece, nor was it completely straight. The wood had settled over the years into the ground, boards had loosened from their original joints, and the weight of soil and snow - to mention nothing of the earthquake - had done their work in nature's attempt to destroy the ship.

Nevertheless, the ship was still largely whole. Certainly, it was no longer sea-worthy, but despite the long epoch through which it had rested on this mountain it had maintained much of its structural integrity. It was at least recognizable as a vast vessel and was most certainly out of place on this mountain. To realize that this was the ship spoken of in Genesis was incredible; the very one which God instructed Noah to build and through which a remnant of humanity and animal life was preserved was here beneath my feet. It was difficult for my mind to conceive of the fact that we had found it or that I was now standing on its very roof. The enormity of what we had discovered still hadn't quite hit me yet, nor the others. We were all still in a state of shock and disbelief.

Wondering what lay inside, I was eager to explore the interior of the Ark, and the opening in the roof beckoned us to enter. Who knew what we might find inside? Motioning towards the entrance before us, I asked the others, "Shall we go in?"

"After you," responded a smiling Arman.

Thankfully, we had brought an additional rope. There was a spot near the hole in the roof which afforded access to both sides of one of the boards; it would be a fine anchor for it. Therefore, I took the rope I had brought from my pack and tied it around the board, tossing the other end through the opening. I then cast my pack down through the opening, hearing a "thump" after less than a second - it wasn't that far to the deck below.

Turning on my flashlight, I held it in my mouth while taking the rope in my hands. I carefully lowered myself through the ragged opening in order to descend onto the deck below. Upon reaching the deck, I shined the light from my flashlight around the area to get my bearings. I was standing on a wooden floor; it was gently inclined due to the lie of the ship on the mountainside. The area ahead of me was higher than my present position, meaning that if I were to go in that direction I would be proceeding to the other end of the ship. Glancing around some more I could see that I had entered into what appeared to be a room. There was an opening in the wall to my left. It was actually a half-opening; there were boards which closed off the lower three feet or so of the exit. It was a doorway with what appeared similar to a baby-gate at the bottom. Stepping over the barrier, I left the room to see what was beyond.

I found myself in a hallway of sorts. It appeared to run the length of the ship, with rooms on either side it. In fact, the entire deck - from what I could tell so far - appeared to be separated into innumerable rooms. Everything was constructed of wood, and the rooms themselves were not completely closed off. Instead, they looked like semi-open animal pens, with low fencing and a small opening leading into each room. The ceilings were high, about ten feet or so.

The wood of the Ark had an ancient patina and was well-aged from the time it had spent here on the mountain. The Bible says that Noah constructed the Ark from "gopher wood." There is no consensus on just what "gopher" means, whether it is a specific type of unknown tree, a construction method involving squaring off the wooden planks, or a way of treating the wood with pitch to seal it against water. Looking at the wood around me, it appeared to be cedar which indeed had been planed so as to make each surface completely square. The wood was darkened as well, likely from a combination of the treatment of pitch as well as extreme age. Perhaps "gopher" should be interpreted as the combination of these three qualities, being a sort of shorthand for wood which was "sea-worthy." I was impressed, and surprised, with the apparent quality of construction. The Ark was in remarkably good shape for its age, although the coldness and altitude of the mountain likely helped to preserve it.

I went back to the room through which I had originally lowered myself into the ship and called up to the others, "It's all clear, you can come down now. Wait 'till you see this."

Martin, Yezras, and then Arman shimmied down the rope and joined me in the room. They turned on their flashlights and looked around to behold what I had first seen. I could see that their eyes were wide in wonder and amazement.

"This is surreal," said Martin.

"What is beyond the door?" asked Yezras.

I answered, "It is a hallway leading to vast numbers of rooms, come and see."

They followed me out of the room and into the

hallway.

"Let's move down the hallway that way - it looks like that probably will lead us to the center of the ship," I said.

We slowly moved forward, past the open doorways.

"There are so many rooms. The animals must have been kept in these," said Arman.

He was right. After passing a few rooms, we ducked into one of them in order to investigate it more closely.

It reminded me of a horse stall with built-in feeding and watering troughs. I could envision Noah's family quickly walking down the hall, checking on the animals, feeding them, and clearing out their waste. In fact, at the far end of the room there was an open hole in the floor against the outer planking, centered mid-length on the wall. It looked like this led to the deck below, and was likely where the waste was scooped or pushed in order to funnel it to the lower decks, potentially to a hold at the very bottom.

I once worked at a horse farm as a teenager and know the effort required to tend to animals. As long as they are healthy, their care requires basic feeding, watering, and waste removal. If they were sick, they required much more care, but sick animals were hard to plan for. Assuming the animals on the Ark were in good health throughout their journey, I could imagine Noah and his family making their daily rounds to all the animal stalls to replenish food and water, with a cleaning of the stalls occurring at a slightly less frequent interval.

"What sort of animal do you think was in this room?" asked Yezras.

"It's hard to tell." I thought for a moment. Would the lighter animals be kept on the upper deck, with progressively heaver animals kept on the lower decks so as to keep the center of gravity of the ship as low as possible? That would help keep the ship stable while at sea. It occurred to me also, though, that many (most?) of the animals were probably smaller juveniles. Bringing younger animals aboard would have helped to lessen the amount of space required to house them as well as the food and water needed to sustain them. It would also have improved the chances that they were healthy.

I pondered Yezras' question about which kind of animal may have been housed in this location. The present stall in which we were could have been home to anything from a large dog to a horse, or maybe multiple animals even. Based on the theory that the top deck was used for lighter animals, I figured that there were probably multiple smaller animals kept in this room, rather than one large animal. Sheep? Dogs? Reptiles? It was probably impossible to say for certain.

"Look at this here," called Arman.

He was on the outside of the room in the hallway. We all exited through the doorway to join him, making sure to step over the low boards which formed the partial, baby-gate-like barrier. Arman pointed us to a carving in the wood on the frame of the room's doorway. It appeared to be some sort of marking. Writing? The marks did appear to consist of multiple letters and have some sort of sensible structure to it - if I could call them "letters," they certainly weren't like normal letters I could recognize. They were definitely symbols, though. Could this carving have recorded the names of the kind, or kinds, of animal kept in the room?

We looked at the door frame of the room directly across the hall and it had what appeared to be identical markings. The room adjacent to both, however, had different markings. Looking around I now noticed that all the rooms appeared to have some sort of writing on them. There were many variations.

I relayed my thoughts to the others. "These inscriptions must be the names of the kinds of animals which were housed in these rooms. Look, these here are the same, but those are different. Noah must have labeled and cataloged everything on the ship."

"Amazing!" said Arman. "I think you are correct.

I only wish we could read the writing to know for sure what was once in these rooms."

We continued down the hallway, past numerous other rooms which were constructed in a similar manner as the one we had just explored. Each had markings on the doorways. I took numerous pictures as we went so as to document our find the best I could; I hoped that if I got clear pictures of the inscriptions that eventually someone could decipher them. As we went down the hallway, room after room we saw a similar pattern of feeding and watering troughs, and waste removal holes. I couldn't wait to see what else we'd discover.

CHAPTER TWENTY-SEVEN

Upper

There were quite a lot of rooms on this deck. This ship must be absolutely gigantic! I knew the dimensions, of course, from the Biblical account, but it was hard to imagine the interior volume and payload capacity without actually seeing the Ark in person. The ship possessed a huge amount of interior storage capacity. We were only on the upper deck, the first we had explored so far - and only cursory at that - yet had already seen so many places for animals to live. With the size of this deck and the number of rooms, it must have housed thousands - possibly tens of thousands - of animals. To think that there were two more deck levels was amazing. They likely contained more space for animals.

We kept progressing down the hall, by this time doing a cursory scan inside each room to see what was inside. It had gotten routine after a while, since all the rooms were built on the same basic pattern; though some were smaller and others larger. There were also a number of them which appeared to contain the remains of cages. For birds or smaller animals, perhaps?

As we moved forward exploring in this fashion, eventually something of special interest caught my eye. I had shined my flashlight into one of the rooms and spied something which seemed worth checking out more fully. Entering the room, I caught sight of clay pots, about ten inches high, most of which were broken, but a few were still - amazingly - intact. I knelt down next to them, picking one up to look at it in more detail.

"Look at these," I called to the others. They were still in the hallway, and entered the room at my call. I showed them the pot I was holding, shining my light upon it so they could see it more clearly.

"Pots, incredible," said Arman.

The others knelt on the floor next to me in order to get a closer look at them as well. The pots appeared to have markings on them, similar to what was written on the door posts. They must have been descriptions of what they once contained. As I thought about the symbols some more, it occurred to me that the script appeared similar to pictures of ancient cuneiform writing which I had seen. Cuneiform was used by the ancient Sumerians thousands of years before Christ. The writing on these pots and doorposts predated that of the Sumerians, although it seemed stylistically linked to it. I imagined that whatever language and writing system Noah had used later developed into Sumerian, following the dispersal of the nations at Babel. This was certainly extremely ancient writing - the precursor to the later more well-known ancient alphabets.

There was a lid on one of the pots. It was stuck closed, either by some sort of sealant or simply due to the effects of time. I pulled at the lid carefully, attempting to open it by successive movements of twisting and pulling. Finally, it budged. I removed the lid and shined my flashlight into the opening of the pot to take a look inside. There appeared to be something dry and granular within. I gently poured out a small amount of the contents onto my palm to look closer. The others, who were still next to me, now stared at the contents of my hand.

"Grain," I said. "This must be over four thousand years old! The cold air and the sealed pot seems to have preserved it. I can't tell for certain what type it is, though. Let's put the lid back on and take some of these sealed pots with us."

"We can each put a pot in our packs. There should be enough room, and our clothing will help cushion and protect them from breaking," said Martin.

The four of us took off our packs and laid them on the floor so that we could store our new-found treasures within them. I tried to bury the pot which was entrusted to me towards the middle and center of my pack so as to provide the most padding around it. After we had all thus stored our artifacts, we put our packs back on, left the room, and headed back to the hall to continue making our way down it.

"Where does all this go?" asked Yezras. "Should we make a plan for our exploration?"

"That is a good idea," answered Arman. "There are supposed to be three decks, according to the Holy Scriptures. Shall we try to find a way down to the next deck below?"

"Yes," I concurred. "I would think that, logically, the center of this deck should likely have stairs or a ladder which will lead us down to the lower deck. Maybe at the fore and aft as well, but we appeared to have entered into the ship near one end, and we didn't see a way down. So, let's try to make our way towards the center, to midship to see what we find."

So on we went, carefully passing through the hallway, stepping over debris while ducking under the occasional drooping timber as we went. It was a tough walk, with the entire ship sloping as it was. We all seemed to walk at an angle, trying to keep our footing while naturally aligning ourselves to counteract gravity's pull. It was almost as if the ship was permanently listing at sea.

The air inside the ship was dry and stale. I could feel the still coldness beginning to seep into my bones. I imagined that the others felt the same.

Only a few days previously we had been warm and in the community of a big city. Now, we were freezing - just the four of us. Four souls treading where no one had walked for thousands of years, on a ship which many believed never existed and which others believed would never be found.

Yet, here we were. Unlikely adventurers and companions, united not by native language or by culture, but by Christ. This truly is the Church: defined not by human customs or decisions, but rather by Christ and the community which he creates around himself. I could feel his presence here among us as we explored this relic which symbolized his grace towards his Church. I felt that he was truly the fifth person in our little party, guiding us onwards, protecting us, watching over us.

These thoughts filled my mind as we went on through the darkened hallway, past yet more rooms where animals had once been sheltered from the flood and preserved through the waters. The Ark had been the instrument of salvation for the Church as well as for life on earth. I prayed that we would make it out of the Ark alive as well.

After walking for a few more minutes we came to a spot where the hallway opened up into a larger area within the deck. It was like a central room or chamber; we must have arrived at the midship section of the ship. I shined my light ahead of us and saw an opening in the floor. Inspecting it, there was a ladder leading down to the next deck beneath us. I call it a ladder, but it was across between a ladder and stairs; simplistic in design, but with a slope so that it was not completely vertical.

There was also a similar ladder which led upwards. I looked at where it ended, but there was no opening, just boards above.

"What do you think that is?" I asked.

"Could it lead to the open windows which were supposed to be on the roof of the Ark?" said Arman.

"Maybe. How do we get up there?" I wondered.

Martin climbed up the ladder and pressed on the boards. "It looks like these will move if we push them upwards hard enough."

"Give it a try," I said.

Martin pushed on the boards. As he did so, dirt fell down on top of us. After some struggle, he was successful in moving the boards out of position, revealing an opening. Light poured through. Martin crawled through the narrow pathway and disappeared.

"Guys, come see this," his disembodied voice came down to us from above.

I ascended the ladder, followed by Yezras and then Arman. We were soon with Martin back on the roof of the Ark. This section of the roof, though, had a covering a few feet high - high enough for us to stand upright. The sides were open. We could see the mountainside and horizon from through the openings. The wind whipped through this covering, dousing us in its coldness.

"These must be the windows which the Bible talks about which were on the roof of the Ark. They provided airflow into the ship when the space through which we crawled was open," I said. "This was likely also the place from which Noah sent out the dove which returned with the olive branch after the flood waters receded."

We thus stood on the very spot at which Noah had received the sign from God that the flood was over and that it was now safe to disembark to begin the repopulation of the world. It marked the end of the difficult journey and the beginning of joyous celebration. I hoped that it symbolized the same for us, that our difficulties were now over and we had but to finish our exploration of the Ark and then return home.

From this vantage point we could see the two peaks of the mountains; Lesser Ararat was to our left towards the South, and Greater Ararat was to our right towards the North. The sun was beginning to set and the first hints of the stars could be seen in the sky. The coming nightfall did not matter to us, though, as long as we were inside the Ark. It shielded us from the winds and, due to the enclosed walls, provided some protection from the freezing air. The darkness of the interior of the ship also necessitated the use of flashlights regardless of whether it was day or night outside.

Therefore, we decided to continue our exploration of the ship rather than making camp for the night.

"Shall we do down to the middle deck?" asked Arman.

"Let's go," I answered.

CHAPTER TWENTY-EIGHT

Middle

The four of us gently descended from the upper windowed roof via the ladder onto the deck from which we had come. We then descended again through the opening in the floor, using the next ladder to reach the deck below. The ladders were in surprisingly decent shape, even though the wood was rickety and worn; at least all the rungs were intact. After reaching the middle deck, we all assembled at the base of the ladder and looked around, our flashlights illuminating the surrounding area.

This deck appeared to be similar to the upper deck in layout and design. The immediate vicinity around the ladder also consisted of a fairly large chamber or central room, and there was a hallway extending out from it, running lengthwise through the ship, with rooms on both sides. Nearby, there was an opening to the deck below and a ladder to reach it. This deck was obviously of the same construction as the upper deck we had explored previously. In fact, it was nearly a mirror image.

"Where should we go?" asked Yezras.

"Should we explore this deck first, then go to the lower deck?" suggested Martin.

"I think that sounds like a good plan. That way we can cover as much of the ship as possible," I said.

Arman agreed. "Yes, after exploring all the decks, we can return to any area we want to look at more fully afterwards. We should follow this hallway and explore the rooms."

Since we were all in agreement, I therefore led us down the hallway. On a whim I picked the direction from whence we had come when we were on the deck above. My intent was that we'd head in that direction, then reverse course, retracing our steps in order to proceed to the opposite end of the hallway. After our exploration was complete, we'd finally return to this central chamber and descend the ladder to the lower deck beneath us. From there we'd investigate the lowest, and presumably final, level of this great ship.

We proceeded down the hall, me leading the way with my flashlight. More rooms greeted us as we went. Many were larger than the rooms on the upper deck, with correspondingly bigger feeding and watering troughs. The animals housed here were obviously from much more sizable species. I went into one of the rooms to take a closer look, stepping over the boards blocking the lower portion of the doorway as I went.   Upon entering the room, I noticed something of interest on the floor. Kneeling, I could see irregular grooves in the wood planking. I felt the wood and the grooves with with my hands, tracing my fingers through the furrows. Amazing!

"These feel like claw marks. Take a look," I said to the others.

The others entered the room after me and knelt beside me, straining to see what I was pointing them to.   After the import of what they were looking at sunk in, they too ran their fingers through the grooves.

"Yes, these were cut here by the claws of large animals!" said Arman.   He seemed excited at the prospect of touching tangible evidence of what had once been kept here.

We exited the room and continued down the hallway. As we went into some of the other rooms, I could see similar markings on the floor and, in some cases, the walls. The evidence that we saw here for the past presence of clawed animals made me think of my hardwood kitchen floors back home; the fact that we had a pet dog would be apparent to anyone who came to our house and saw our floors. Likewise, the animals which had been on this Ark had left similar evidence in the wood for all time. Now here we were seeing this physical attestation of the Ark's previous inhabitants for ourselves.

We left the room and continued our journey through the hall. As we did so, the sheer size of this ship hit me as simply magnificent. We encountered room after room capable of storing numerous animals, both large and small. The immensity of the interior was beyond comprehension. We had already explored two decks filled with rooms, and the deck below was likely to be the same. This ship certainly possessed the ability to carry a huge amount of cargo.

My mind transported me back to Noah's day, imagining he and his family walking through the hallways of the Ark. They would have passed room after room filled with life. They would have heard grunting, roaring, chirping, and all manner of sounds from their charges. They would have smelled the mixed array of mammals, reptiles, birds, and others. It must have been quite an experience, and the sheer amount of animals which would have been onboard was incredible. In fact, the number of rooms in the ship gave sense to the immense amount of work required of Noah and his family to care for those entrusted to them by God Himself. While the four of us were overwhelmed with the enormity of the ship, it occurred to me that we were half the number of Noah's party of eight. That was still not many people to tend a ship of this size. However, I supposed that having all the rooms consist of a similar pattern and connecting them by a long hallway on each deck made it easier and faster to check on and care for all the animals. They likely had a daily schedule to cover every area of each deck to make their activities as efficient as possible.

We continued to pass by a number of additional rooms, peering inside as we went, our flashlights illuminating the floor and walls. We saw the same pattern in each room: feeding and watering troughs, waste drainage holes, and the occasional marks on the floors. Soon we would be at the end of the hall and would begin doubling-back to the central chamber so that we could continue our exploration with the lower deck.

Without warning, I felt the wood decking underneath my feet give way. A loud crack and I was thrust into darkness below.

CHAPTER TWENTY-NINE

Lower

"Are you alright?!" Three voices from the deck above rang out simultaneously.

I was on my back, having just had the wind knocked out of me by the impact from the fall. I gasped for breath.

The others continued to yell down to me. I was barely able to speak, as I was still trying to regain my breath. It took me a few seconds until I was finally able to say, "Yes, I think I found the next deck." I had fallen into the hallway of the lower deck; it must have been about an eight foot fall. Thankfully, I seemed ok and had managed to hold onto my flashlight during the fall. I used it now to look around to get my bearings and to see what was nearly. More rooms. How many rooms could this ship possibly have?! Yet, these seemed slightly different.

I yelled up to the others, "I'm going to look

around. Do you guys want to catch a ladder to get down here?"

"Yes, we will do that. We will head back midship to use the ladder there and then come meet you where you are," answered Arman.

I could hear them walking on the decking above me as they proceeded back towards the middle of the ship from where we had all started out together. It would take them a few minutes to get back to midship, descend to the deck on which I now was, and then proceed to find their way to me. Due to the distance and their haste, they would be worn out by the time they got to me. I chuckled to myself at the thought that I was lucky for having found a shortcut through the floor.

Where to go until they arrived? I didn't just want to sit and wait for them, so I decided upon a room to enter nearby. This one was different than the others we had encountered on the upper two decks. It had no boards blocking the lower portion of the doorway; it was instead open all the way. Upon entering the room, I saw that it looked like a store room rather than an animal stall. Lining the far wall there were ancient wooden crates, almost like modern military foot lockers (but without the lock). I approached one of the crates and lifted its heavy wooden lid off of it. Shining my light inside I saw that there were the sparse remains of what appeared to be more grain. Amazing, I thought, that this has been preserved here for so long. Perhaps this was a different type of grain than what we had found on the upper deck in the pots. Or maybe this was a central store, and the pots were used to ferry grain from here to the animals. That seemed to make sense, but it was hard to tell for certain. I took a number of pictures of both the interior and exterior of the crate I had opened, but decided to leave the others untouched so that they could be more carefully studied later. I also took as many pictures as I could of the room itself. The general low light level in the interior of the ship made getting quality photographs difficult, however. Even with my camera's flash, the image quality was less than ideal.

Leaving the room, I proceeded to an adjacent room to look inside. It also contained crates which had presumably stored additional food for the duration of the flood. This pattern was repeated in more of the nearby rooms which contained yet further crates. In a few of the rooms I also found large, rounded pottery jars with lids. Maybe these were to store liquids, like fresh water or wine? I opened one and could see that the inside was stained red; I surmised that this must have been for wine. I opened another and saw the same red stains. I took a jar, placing it in my backpack to take back with us after our expedition was done.

Following my exploration of the rooms in my immediate vicinity, I decided to head down the hall towards the middle of the ship in order to meet my fellow explorers. I felt that I had exhausted the novelties of the rooms in the area in which I had fallen and wanted to see what lay ahead. Progressing down the hall, therefore, I began to observe yet more rooms as I went. Some were similar to the storage rooms I had just explored. However, others were larger and had obviously housed quite huge animals. Entering a few of them I could see the feeding and watering troughs as well as claw marks like I had observed in the rooms on the deck above.

I kept going down the hall, peering into rooms as I went. More and more were animal stalls, although I did still encounter the occasional storage area. I figured that it made sense that the largest animals were kept near the center of the lowest deck. Doing so would ensure that the center of gravity was low and that the ship was stable.

As I approached midship I heard voices ahead. They were muffled, but I knew that it was the others (who else would be here?), finally having made their way down to this deck.

"Martin, can you hear me?" I called out.

"Yes, Dad, come here and look at this." Martin's voice reverberated through the wooden hallway.

I rushed ahead and after a short distance could make out a form in the distance. As I got closer, I saw Martin waving to me, motioning me to come to him. He was near the ladder which led from this deck to the deck above. It appeared that they had all gotten distracted by something upon making their descent down the ladder. As I approached, I saw that this level was similar to the upper two in that there was a large open area near the ladder, with the hallway leading into it. Martin was standing next to a room which connected directly to the open area.

"What is it?" I asked upon reaching him.

"You have to see this room," he answered as he led me inside.

Arman and Yezras were already within. Upon entering, I surveyed a large room with what looked like wooden cots built into the sides of the wall. The cots were low, only about a foot high and probably no more than two feet wide and six feet long. Indexing from the entrance, there were two cots on the leftward wall, two on the rightward wall, and four on the longer wall directly opposite the entryway to the room. The cots were old and tattered by time, but still largely intact and definitely recognizable as sleeping cots.

"There are…" I started to say.

"Eight of them, I know," Martin finished my sentence.

"This was where where Nuh and his family slept," said Arman.

It was quite a sight to see the very place where

Noah's family had lived aboard the Ark during the time of the flood. They spent about a year on the ship, so probably whittled away many a darkened night in this space. Looking around the room some more I could see what appeared to be vents cut into the wood of the ceiling of the room, presumably leading up and eventually outward to the sides of the hull. They must have been used both for allowing fresh air in and stale air out.

Arman and Yezras motioned for me to look more closely at the far wall of the room, shining their flashlights on it to illuminate what they wished me to see.

Amazing.

Above the cots were vertical marks, like someone had been counting days by carving them into the wooden wall. I tried counting them quickly, but Arman provided the answer before I could finish.

"Forty marks," said Arman.

"The number of days of rain in the time of Noah's flood," I answered.

"Yes," he said. "And look over here."

He shined his light onto another section of the wall. I saw more marks, but this time I knew that there were too many for me to quickly count, so I waited for Arman to give me the answer as I knew he would if I waited long enough.

"One Hundred Fifty," he said after a short silence.

"The duration of the flood," I said.

"This is quite remarkable," said Yezras.

I nodded in agreement. To see these marks was like stepping back in time, to the time of Noah. It was almost like he and his family were here with us as we explored the place where they had lived for the duration of the flood. We were in the midst of their living quarters, with the cots on which they slept against the walls and the evidence for their presence scratched upon the walls. I could envision Noah and his family marking off the days of the rain and the days of the flood in the wood. Day after day they went to the wall and carved another line to keep track of the period of their journey. Did they wonder if the waters would ever subside? Were they worried that they were the last people alive on earth? Did they ponder how they would begin again once, or even if, the flood finally ended?

Then, I noticed something on the wall to my right. I couldn't quite make it out; all I could tell was that there was some sort of image there. The others hadn't seen it yet, so I shined my light onto it to reveal it to us all. It was a painting, or wall mural more appropriately. Of eight people! An older man and woman and three sets of younger men and women were in it, only their heads and faces being depicted.

This was, I assumed, a portrait of Noah and his family. He and his wife were the older couple and their sons and daughters-in-law were the younger couples. The entire family was depicted here, painted by one of them long ago. The colors were still fairly well preserved, if faint, and the quality was actually quite good. It was not "photo-realistic," but it did remind me of the paintings I had seen in old Roman-era villas from Pompeii. It was a respectable talent who had created this.

I took pictures of all the walls with my camera, doing my best to capture as much detail as I could in the limited lighting. The others assisted by shining their flashlights on the wall.

We exited this room we had dubbed the "living quarters" and explored the other rooms which also opened out directly into the central area around the ladder. One of these appeared to be a place for eating. There was a low wooden table built into the center of the floor. On the far wall there was another, smaller doorway which led into another room; we crossed over the table and entered in.

We immediately saw a stone hearth against one wall, with vents cut into the ceiling above for airflow. Nearby were a couple discarded metal pots, apparently of bronze, but long since tarnished. The family must have prepared and cooked their food in this room and then eaten their meals together in the adjoining room. We had apparently discovered their "kitchen" and "dining room."

There was a smaller alcove directly connected to this one as well. Upon entering, we saw that it was completely empty. We could not determine the use of this room for certain, but I surmised that it had been used for storing the immediately-needed cooking supplies and ingredients. I could imagine the family using it as a pantry of sorts. They would have pulled provisions from some of the larger rooms we had previously encountered in order to re-stock the pantry as needed, then used the supplies in the pantry for their meals.

We proceeded out of the pantry back to the kitchen and then returned to the dining room. In our haste to explore the adjoining rooms we had not properly surveyed the dining room when we had first entered it. We therefore took the opportunity to inspect it more closely now. The illumination from our flashlights revealed hints of something on the walls.

CHAPTER THIRTY

Illustrations

"Look at this," I said to the others, shining my light on the wall so they could more clearly make out what I had noticed.

"Are those paintings?" asked Martin.

Arman and Yezras moved closer to see. Then they began to inspect the other walls of the room.

"These are more murals," said Arman.

His son finished his thought, "They are like the one we had seen in the other room - in the living quarters."

Arman and Martin were correct. There were a series of painted murals on the walls of this dining room. These murals were different, however, than the one in the other room which depicted Noah and his family. The ones in this room appeared to illustrate natural scenes and landscapes. Upon closer inspection, we realized that they were actually something even more profound and meaningful. These scenes actually depicted the events of the flood itself in successive murals around the walls of the dining room. When standing at the far end of the low dining table, it was obvious that the images began on the left wall and proceeded clockwise around the room. They were all arranged according to the chronology of the flood such that each sequential picture portrayed a moment in time which followed the one before. Examining all the images in this manner, we found that we could visually follow the Biblical account of the flood. I documented everything with my camera the best I could.

The first mural in the series was a depiction of people, presumably Noah and his family, building the Ark. It showed the events recorded in Genesis 6:14-16 as God instructed Noah on what to construct:

Make yourself an ark of gopher wood. Make rooms in the ark, and cover it inside and out with pitch. This is how you are to make it: the length of the ark three hundred cubits, its breadth fifty cubits, and its height thirty cubits. Make a roof for the ark, and finish it to a cubit above, and set the door of the ark in its side. Make it with lower, second, and third decks.

In this scene the ship was in the background, partially constructed, with the ribs still visible due to the lack of planking in certain spots. What appeared to be hand tools and A-frame benches were in the foreground. The people were depicted in various stages of the act of construction: some working with wooden planks on the A-frames, others near the ship itself, and others carrying supplies. The Ark itself had three visible decks, able to be seen through the open planking, with a small cover at the top over an opening of windows. Presumably, this was for venting and access to fresh air. The four of us had explored sections of these three decks, along with the top windowed area.

Then, the next mural in the series was a depiction of vast numbers of animals coming to the Ark from all directions. They were heading to the Ark in pairs, with some types of animals arranged in seven pairs. These were presumably the "clean" animals which God had instructed Noah to bring extras of onboard. This was done according to God's instructions recorded in Genesis 6:19 and 7:2-3:

And of every living thing of all flesh, you shall bring two of every sort into the ark to keep them alive with you. They shall be male and female... Take with you seven pairs of all clean animals, the male and his mate, and a pair of the animals that are not clean, the male and his mate, and seven pairs of the birds of the heavens also, male and female, to keep their offspring alive on the face of all the earth.

The ship was shown in a completed state, with a ramp leading up to a wide and tall door in the midst of the lower deck. Noah and his family appeared to be ushering the animals into their new haven aboard the ramp and through the ship's door. Onlookers were depicted nearby with what appeared to be scoffing faces and postures. The ship certainly looked out of place, lying as it was on a grassy plain with no water in sight.

Beside this mural was the next in the series. This one depicted the beginning of the flood itself. It showed rain falling upon the Ark which was still sitting on the plain, but now closed up for the duration of the coming flood as described in Genesis 7:11-12:

In the six hundredth year of Noah's life, in the second month, on the seventeenth day of the month, on that day all the fountains of the great deep burst forth, and the windows of the heavens were opened. And rain fell upon the earth forty days and forty nights.

Portions of the surrounding plain were just starting to be covered with water, and the grasses were depicted as being partially submerged; however, the Ark had not yet begun to float. People were coming to the Ark, presumably to be let in, but Noah and his family - along with the animals - were already sealed safely inside. There would be no haven for those who had rejected the Ark.

Next to this one, there was another picture. The waters had now covered all of the surrounding land, and the Ark was completely floating on the water; no earth could be seen, it was just the Ark and endless water. Seeing the bleakness of this depiction, and knowing that one of those aboard had painted it made we further contemplate the thoughts of Noah and his family during the flood. Did they wonder if the waters would ever subside? The picture here certainly looked dire. The entire earth was inundated, leaving just the Ark as the instrument of salvation for the small family inside and the animals in their care. From Genesis 7:17-20:

The flood continued forty days on the earth. The waters increased and bore up the ark, and it rose high above the earth. The waters prevailed and increased greatly on the earth, and the ark floated on the face of the waters. And the waters prevailed so mightily on the earth that all the high mountains under the whole heaven were covered. The waters prevailed above the mountains, covering them fifteen cubits deep.

The next mural shifted the scene. No longer was the outside of the Ark and the surrounding landscape - or lack thereof - shown. Instead, the interior was depicted. The painting showed a subset of the interior of the ship, revealing what the areas we had walked through during our exploration must have looked like in the time of Noah. Animals were shown in their stalls, with Noah's family distributing food and tending to them. Various kinds of animals were portrayed, including elephants, birds, horses, lizards, and others.

Only Noah was left, and those who were with him in the ark (Genesis 7:23).

The following picture shifted the scene yet again to show the outside of the Ark, with a focus on the top, windowed deck with the cover. This was the highest point of the ship which we had explored earlier. In this image, a man was looking at a bird which had a branch in its beak. This was an illustration of Noah and the dove which the Bible says was sent out by Noah and returned with an olive branch after the waters subsided. It was a sign that it was now safe to disembark from the Ark:

And the dove came back to him in the evening, and behold, in her mouth was a freshly plucked olive leaf. So Noah knew that the waters had subsided from the earth. Then he waited another seven days and sent forth the dove, and she did not return to him anymore (Genesis 8:11-12).

The next picture depicted the disembarkation of the inhabitants of the Ark as recorded in Genesis 8:18-19:

So Noah went out, and his sons and his wife and his sons' wives with him. Every beast, every creeping thing, and every bird, everything that moves on the earth, went out by families from the ark.

This time the Ark was shown from the outside again. It was lying on a sloped plain, nestled between two mountain peaks. This was the saddle between the "Mountains of Ararat," the very place where we now stood. The door to the Ark was open, the ramp was in place, and endless swaths of animals were descending down the slopes onto the plain to find their new homes, with Noah's family shepherding them away from the ship.

The final picture depicted eight people around an altar; Noah and his family worshipping the Lord who had preserved them through the Ark:

Then Noah built an altar to the LORD and took some of every clean animal and some of every clean bird and offered burnt offerings on the altar (Genesis 8:20).

Above them were blue, cloudless skies, with a rainbow above:

And God said, "This is the sign of the covenant that I make between me and you and every living creature that is with you, for all future generations: I have set my bow in the cloud, and it shall be a sign of the covenant between me and the earth. When I bring clouds over the earth and the bow is seen in the clouds, I will remember my covenant that is between me and you and every living creature of all flesh. And the waters shall never again become a flood to destroy all flesh. When the bow is in the clouds, I will see it and remember the everlasting covenant between God and every living creature of all flesh that is on the earth." God said to Noah, "This is the sign of the covenant that I have established between me and all flesh that is on the earth" (Genesis 9: 12 - 17).

I reflected upon the imagery contained within these murals. In depicting the events of the flood, they illustrated both God's wrath and His mercy. His wrath is revealed through His judgment against sin and His resultant actions to destroy a world which was completely corrupted by it. His mercy, though, is revealed through His grace in saving Noah and his family from the flood and using them, and the Ark, as the instrument through which a remnant of life on earth was saved.

However, these murals also conveyed something even more far-reaching. They expressed the truth that salvation is much more encompassing and meaningful than just an individual person's connection with God. Salvation involves being brought into a community which has been reconciled with God as well as the restoration of creation and a new life within it. For that is what these flood scenes ultimately depicted: those saved by God's grace and made His people entering into a new, restored creation.

It is no surprise then that the Church has traditionally made connections between the Christian faith and Noah's Ark. This is seen most prominently in baptism, as I had observed many days ago at the purported tomb of Noah in Nakhchivan. The historic design of the baptismal font is eight-sided, and this contains a deep symbolism. In the beginning, God brought everything into existence in six days; the Father spoke forth His Word to create, and His Spirit hovered over the created waters to bring order and sanctification to what had been made. God rested on the seventh day after completing His work. Then, the eighth day was the dawn of the new week, heralding the beginning of the first full week of the new creation. Similarly, Noah and his family were eight souls saved across the waters on the Ark and brought into a new creation of sorts which had been cleansed by the water. Jesus Christ himself rose from the dead on the eighth day, Sunday, the first day of a new week, beginning the ushering in of a new creation that one day will no longer be tainted by sin, death, or evil.

The Church has always made the connection between baptism, the number eight, and the Ark for all these reasons. In fact, the Church has continually taught that in baptism God is recreating the one being baptized, bringing him out of captivity to a fallen world and into God's reign instead. The one baptized becomes a new creation through the power of God's Word attached to the water and is given God's promise that one day he or she will also bodily rise from the dead to inherit the new, restored creation which Jesus Christ is bringing with him at his return. The baptized is thus cleansed with the waters and brought into the first fruits of the new creation, having been reconciled with God and incorporated into the community of the Church.

Therefore, the Ark we had found here on these mountains was not the end, nor even the beginning of God's plans for humanity. Yet, it is illustrative of God's saving actions for not only humanity, but for all creation. For the sake of Noah and his family - the entire Church on earth at that time - God preserved life on this earth. On the Ark, God sustained life and brought them into a new world across the waters with which He baptized the whole earth to cleanse it.

* * *

The Ark is therefore illustrative of the Church herself. God is preserving life for the sake of the Church and is not destroying His creation, but rather restoring it. One day it will be restored to the original perfection in which He had created it, before Adam and Eve brought sin, death, and evil into the world through their sin. In fact, the Bible depicts this restoration in the Revelation given to St. John. The Book of Revelation reveals what it will be like when all things are finally restored to perfection, and the Church - illustrated in the form of the beautiful New Jerusalem - inherits the earth:

Then I saw a new heaven and a new earth, for the first heaven and the first earth had passed away, and the sea was no more. And I saw the holy city, new Jerusalem, coming down out of heaven from God, prepared as a bride adorned for her husband. And I heard a loud voice from the throne saying, "Behold, the dwelling place of God is with man. He will dwell with them, and they will be his people, and God himself will be with them as their God. He will wipe away every tear from their eyes, and death shall be no more, neither shall there be mourning nor crying nor pain anymore, for the former things have passed away" (Revelation 21: 1 - 4).

Everything is thus finished and made perfect at the end when Christ returns and resurrects our bodies to bring us into the new creation. As a sign of the realization of God's promises, the rainbow which God had shown Noah in Genesis finally comes full circle in the vision given to John in Revelation:

> *... before me was a throne in heaven with someone sitting on it. And the one who sat there had the appearance of jasper and ruby. A rainbow that shone like an emerald encircled the throne (Revelation 4:3 NIV).*

Thus, what God had been promising throughout the ages reaches its zenith as the rainbow is completed, revealing that God's plans and promises for eternal life in a restored creation finally come to fruition on the day of the resurrection when Christ returns.

This was the real treasure I had found on this mountain. It was a reminder of the full scope of God's plans for His creation. Salvation was not just a matter between me and God. Nor was it just an issue of God's relationship with humanity. I had gotten glimpses of this truth throughout the previous days of our journey to find the Ark. I had felt the community of the Church among Arman, Yezras, Martin, and myself. Together we had seen the images depicting God's salvation of life on earth through the Ark. This was all a foreshadowing and token of what God has in store for His creation at Christ's return as he brings salvation with him. This is a salvation in the fullest, truest sense of the word: God restoring all the world, making a new creation, and bringing His Church - the true Ark - into it to live in peace forever.

Whatever else we had found on this vast ship paled in comparison to these truths which God had shown me on the journey. It truly was the real discovery.

Now we must all find our way out of here to go tell others what had been revealed to us. After all, was this not the mission of the Church?

CHAPTER THIRTY-ONE

Epilogue

It had been an arduous, but rewarding adventure. Now it was over.

We had spent the night on the Ark and then continued our exploration of it on the following day, taking many more pictures as we went. The rest of the ship was much the same as I had previously related; room after room, some for animals and others for storage. After another night on the ship we departed and headed back down the mountain the fastest we could. We decided to take the easiest route down which we could find, even though that meant we ultimately found ourselves at the foot of the mountains a couple miles away from our original base camp. We had wanted to return to the base camp in order to pick up the supplies we had left there before our ascent. Thus, we made the trek back to that location and there again spent the evening. Early the following morning we made the hike back to Aralik to reunite with Arman's car. Thankfully, but unsurprisingly, it was still there and in one piece. We happily loaded our gear inside and headed back to Nakhchivan, having to again pay the border officials "fees" to leave Turkey and reenter Azerbaijan.

Back in Nakhchivan, Arman, Yezras, Martin, and I shared thoughts over a few beers while relaxing in a small cafe. After our return, we had alerted the American news media, sending some pictures as evidence of our find, and were soon contacted by various government agencies, including those of Turkey, Armenia, and Azerbaijan. The most pressing contact, though, came from the United States government. U.S. authorities were keenly interested in what had been found in the mountains of Turkey, a NATO member and ally, by US citizens and their foreign companions.

We had met extensively with representatives from the U.S. State Department in Azerbaijan, showing them the artifacts we had collected and photos we had taken. They promised to mount a recovery operation in conjunction with the Turkish authorities. The wheels of government turn slowly, however, and it was not long before the heavy winter snows began to fall on the mountains and another larger aftershock of the original earthquake disturbed the area. These events conspired together to once again conceal the Ark from view. It now awaits its rediscovery by a future generation at some later date known only to God. We had our pictures and artifacts, but many who read the press reports accused us of forgery and fraud. There were a few who believed, though.

I suppose it would have been much the same, though, had the world seen the Ark with its own eyes. Many would have dismissed it, explaining it away as some sort of "natural" occurrence, even if odd. Others would have discounted it as the work of some ancient mariner who survived a local flood. Those of faith would have believed, of course. But then they already did. Faith trusts God's Word and needs no proof. Thus, for the rest of the world to have seen the Ark would have changed little in actual fact.

In the end, then, our discovery was somewhat innocuous. We had found the Ark, but could neither prove it to a doubting world nor did the believing Church require the proof which we had found.

Maybe, after all, this is the point of all this. I thought back to the time of Christ. The early Church saw Christ resurrected from the dead. Many others saw him as well, or heard the reports of his resurrection. Yet, some still did not believe. However, for the Church no proof was necessary; it took God's Word on faith. In our own time still, the Church lives through faith and trusts in the veracity of the testimony of the Apostles which has been handed down to us. We have not seen Christ's resurrection, yet believe due to the Apostolic witness.

Was this why the Ark had been hidden for so long? Did God know that us finding proof of the existence of the Ark would made no difference in the end? Was this the truth He wanted to reveal to us: that those who trust in God would do so regardless of whether or not the Ark was found, while those who rejected God would continue to do so, even if they confronted the Ark face-to-face. It was much the same with Christ as well.

Arman, Yezras, Martin, and myself had seen the Ark face-to-face and walked among its mysteries. Yet, it occurred to me that, ultimately, we did not need this. We already believed in Christ. We were already part of the Church. We did not need proof. Why, then, had God granted us the honor and privilege of seeing the Ark? Did He grant this to us since we did already believe and so would take some greater truth away from the discovery? What were we meant to understand by this?

Perhaps the message we were meant to receive, and proclaim to those who would listen, is that the Church is one in Christ, throughout time and geography. The four of us were united in Christ - part of the Church together, part of Christ's own body - despite our differences of culture, ethnicity, nation, and native language. Christ joined us together as part of his Church whom he has died and risen for.

Likewise, we were also united in faith with Noah and his family. They were part of the Old Testament Church: eight faithful souls who believed God and were saved through this faith on account of

God's grace. They heeded His warnings and trusted in His promises. They placed their hopes in Him and the wooden Ark of His salvation. We had seen the remnants of their vessel which carried them across the waters to salvation. Likewise, we - in our own time - have been baptized in the waters of the font and are carried across the ark of the Church to salvation. We are united with them by Christ within the Church as well, having been redeemed through the wooden cross.

We have not yet met Noah and his family in person, but one day we will. At the resurrection when Christ returns, the four of us here in this cafe, our families, Noah and his family, and all the rest of the Church of all times and places will stand together before our Lord and inherit the restored creation.

After this I looked, and behold, a great multitude that no one could number, from every nation, from all tribes and peoples and languages, standing before the throne and before the Lamb, clothed in white robes, with palm branches in their hands, and crying out with a loud voice, "Salvation belongs to our God who sits on the throne, and to the Lamb!" (Revelation 7: 9 - 10)

On that day, our hopes and faith will be fulfilled, and we will finally receive the inheritance which our Heavenly Father has promised us, Christ won for us, and the Holy Spirit safeguards for us. We will receive eternal life in a perfect world. It is, however, something we have to wait for. Noah and his family had to wait many months for the waters to begin to subside and for the Ark to rest on the mountain where we had found it. Now, long since dead, their bodies wait for the resurrection, as will ours some day.

As Arman, Yezras, Martin, and I finished our drinks we began to say our goodbyes. Emotion flowed over us all, knowing that we would not likely see one another again in this mortal life. We shook hands and hugged each other.

Then, Arman stood upright and solemnly declared on behalf of Yezras and himself, "We shall see you again at the resurrection."

"Yes," I answered, "Yes, indeed."

And we most certainly will.